"You're not paying attention, my lady," Willem chided, his breath warm on her cheek.

"Oh, I am paying attention—but not to the music."

His familiar chuckle rumbled deep in his chest. "Play it through once more."

She played it again—better than before. "I think you must be part magician—so artfully do you instruct me."

"It is *you* who have enchanted me—with your skill and beauty," he whispered, then rose to fetch a chair near hers. "Let us try the Schwarzwald tune, but without the lyrics. I would speak with you without being overheard."

Margarethe nodded and began strumming the simple song about the Black Forest, where she had spent her early years with her father and mother and a little sister she barely remembered. There were only a few memories of the call of the cuckoo bird, and running on forest paths, gilded by slivers of sunlight through the thick canopy of trees, and playing and hide and seek with neighboring children. "What would you speak with me about?" she asked with a sinking heart.

"Lord Einhard has asked me to compose new music to celebrate. . .a certain occasion."

"What occasion is that?"

"Your betrothal."

She stumbled over a chord. "My betrothal? But when? And to whom?"

"He mentioned May Day, I believe." Willem turned to regard her in surprise. "And you have no notion who it is to be?"

"I only know who *I* want it to be." She fought the lump in her throat, then concentrated on her playing.

KATHLEEN SCARTH writes about what she loves—music and the Lord. Like her heroine in *For a Song*, Kathleen can sing and play a variety of instruments. She also loves history and chose Germany, a setting not often seen in historical novels, for the location of her first published work.

For a Song

Kathleen Scarth

Heartsong Presents

For Franci, my daughter and friend,
who is always asking for more chapters

A note from the author:
I love to hear from my readers! You may write to me at
the following address: **Kathleen Scarth**
Author Relations
PO Box 719
Uhrichsville, OH 44683

ISBN 1-57748-281-6

FOR A SONG

Cover illustration by Lauraine Bush.

PRINTED IN THE U.S.A.

one

Adlerschloss
Southwestern Bavaria
1327 A.D.

An untimely March snow melted in the thin morning sunshine as Margarethe hugged herself for warmth at the open castle window. Though she wore a blue wool tunic over her woolen smock and a purple velvet surcoat over that, it was still much too cold to be comfortable. But Father Bernard had not yet arrived for her lessons, and she refused to sit by the fire like some old village woman at her spinning wheel.

This third-story window in the room where she had studied since she was seven offered a view of both bailey and countryside. She knew every outbuilding, the stables, the gardens, the great round towers atop crenellated walls. Uncle Einhard was quite proud of his castle, built in the modern style in this, the fourteenth century since the coming of Christ.

She could see beyond the walls to rolling hills and forests, fertile farmlands stirring to life in spite of their light blanket of white. Somewhere out there—over the horizon and many furlongs distant—there was fighting and bloodshed. But here in her own corner of Bavaria, the seasons came and went on schedule, undisturbed by man's foolish disputes over boundaries and borders.

Margarethe left off her musings, for she had spotted something more interesting nearer at hand. A kitchen maid, plump as a Christmas pudding, stood against the stone wall by the brewery door. She glanced up, her mouth dropping open as she met Margarethe's eye, then took her hand from the folds of her russet cloak to reveal a large snowball. Margarethe grinned and put a finger to her lips, signaling her complicity. The maid resumed her vigil in anticipation of the ambush.

At that moment Margarethe heard Father Bernard's ponderous approach through the rushes in the hallway, and tucked a stray wisp of hair back under her cap. She turned and beckoned him over to the window. He joined her just in time to see the kitchen maid hurl her snowball at the brewer.

It struck the fellow on the shoulder, and he started after the maid, but slipped in the mud, flailing his arms and legs to avoid a fall. The maid's laughter rang out, rising to drift through the open shutters and mingle with Margarethe's and Father Bernard's. Hearing them, the ruddy-faced brewer looked up and gave a jaunty little wave.

Father Bernard saluted him and turned to Margarethe, who closed the shutters and drew the draperies against the chill. "A good morning to you, my lady. Pray forgive my tardiness. I was detained by your uncle." He bowed and smiled.

Margarethe's breath caught in her throat at the sadness clouding his dear old face. She did not protest when Father Bernard took her arm and led her over to the study table near the fire. "Did my uncle say something that would lead you to believe he is thinking of. . .ending my time as your student soon?"

Father Bernard was exceedingly gentle as he seated her. "He is considering several matrimonial prospects for you now that you have seen sixteen summers."

Margarethe sighed and settled into her chair at the spot where she had studied for nearly nine years. "Then I am glad it's too muddy to send messengers to the Schwarzwald. Uncle Einhard can't arrange for me to marry anyone without my parents' approval."

Her parents, whom she had seen but a few times since being fostered here at the age of seven to study musci with her Aunt Mechthild, seemed so far away. She understood why they had visited so seldom: with the floods of the past few years, the road were near to being bogs. And even in fair weather, there was always the threat of highwaymen and thieves, or soldiers marching to join "Otto's war," as he uncle called it. As it was, she had grown to love her aunt and uncle dearly, as well as her old teacher and a certain other.

"Your family loves you far too much not to choose wisely for you." Father Bernard regarded her kindly, tapping a finger on the sturdy oak table, then continued. "Your Uncle Otto will be here for supper tonight."

"He is no uncle of mine!" Margarethe scowled, then quickly sobered. "I am torn, Father. Should I pray that the mud lingers so that messengers can't get through? Or should I pray that the mud dries up so that Lord Otto and his sons will stop bothering about me and go back to their silly war?"

There was a note of reproval in the priest's voice. "Any of Lord Otto's sons would make a fine match for you, Margarethe. All hold lands nearby."

"And holding land is vital to a match, I know." She could not restrain her bitterness and was relieved when her old tutor opened a book to begin their studies.

After the Latin lesson, they reviewed the medicinal properties of borage, peppermint, and loosestrife. Margarethe was reminded once again of the passage of time. She had seen a few daffodils this morning blooming bravely in the snow by the herb garden.

Father Bernard took his leave early. "Willem has asked for extra time with you today," he said, while Margarethe carefully schooled her face to a look of disinterest. "I believe he has in mind practicing a new song to entertain your uncle's supper guests."

"Very well, Father." At the mention of the music instructor's name, Margarethe had felt her pulse quicken. "I am looking forward to our history lesson tomorrow."

As soon as he left, she pulled a strand of hair from her cap, curling it around one finger, then shook out her surcoat over her tunic. Pinching her cheeks for color, she hurried to fetch her lute and was tuning it when Willem appeared, his steps silent except for the whisper of the rushes.

She smiled up at him, and he held her gaze as he bowed over her hand. He was wearing a new green tunic in a shade that brought out the blue of his eyes by contrast. "Good morning, my lady. I see that you are already hard at work."

"Certainly, good sir," she replied, allowing herself a slightly flirtatious tone. "I am weary with studying and, were my relative not coming tonight, would enjoy playing only a few simple tunes today."

Willem shook his head. "Alas, it is not to be. Lord Einhard advised me that a special song was in order for this evening." He slanted her a knowing look. "I thought we might introduce our latest composition."

She sighed, dropping the banter for the moment. "I suppose. I do wish you'd let me play some easier part for the instrumental passage, though. My fingers aren't wise to it yet." She looked down at her lute to hide her smile.

Willem came and sat beside her with his homespun bag of wind instruments. "It is you who composed the words and the melody. And since that passage is my only contribution to the piece, do let it remain." He dropped his gaze to her hands on the lute. "Those fingers may be soft, my lady, but they are nimble and skillful beyond your admission."

She felt a blush stain her cheeks, and hastened to tune the last string. "Besides, no one will notice any mistakes as long as you don't grimace."

Margarethe laughed.

Willem strummed his own instrument, and they played some chords to warm their fingers before applying themselves to the new song. It was a love song, to be performed as a duet, and it would have been most pleasant were it not for that tricky part.

They ran through the tune several times. Then, tiring of the tedious exercise, Margarethe grinned mischievously. "I think I need your help with this, Willem. Can you show me once more how to get my two hands to work together?"

He cocked an eyebrow and glanced out the doorway. "I would have thought by now, you'd be able to do this quite easily." His look was one of amusement before he tiptoed to the thick timber door and pulled it closed.

Coming around behind her chair, Willem bent over, putting his hands over hers and guiding her through the intricate passage so she could get a feel for the places where the fingering changes intersected with the plucking pattern. Margarethe, savoring his closeness, missed a few notes.

"You're not paying attention, my lady," Willem chided, his breath warm on her cheek.

"Oh, I am paying attention—but not to the music."

His familiar chuckle rumbled deep in his chest. "Play it through once more."

She played it again—better than before. "I think you must be part magician—so artfully do you instruct me."

"It is *you* who have enchanted me—with your skill and beauty," he whispered, then rose to fetch a chair near hers. "Let us try the Schwarzwald tune, but without the lyrics. I would speak with you without being overheard."

Margarethe nodded and began strumming the simple song about the Black Forest, where she had spent her early years with her father and mother and a little sister she barely remembered. There were only a few memories of the call of the cuckoo bird, and running on forest paths, gilded by slivers of sunlight through the thick canopy of trees, and playing and hide and seek with neighboring children. "What would you speak with me about?" she asked with a sinking heart.

"Lord Einhard has asked me to compose new music to celebrate. . .a certain occasion."

"What occasion is that?"

"Your betrothal."

She stumbled over a chord. "My betrothal? But when? And to whom?"

"He mentioned May Day, I believe." Willem turned to regard her in surprise. "And you have no notion who it is to be?"

"I only know who I *want* it to be." She fought the lump in her throat, then concentrated on her playing.

They played without further conversation for a full chorus before Willem broke the somber silence so at odds with the cheerful song. "Though I am a nobleman, I have no prospect of acquiring land. My brother is not in poor health, nor is he given to war. I cannot ask him to divide the land with me, for there is not enough for both of us. And I am a second son, as you know, and there is no remedy for that."

"Second sons often end up as priests or monks." In this case, Margarethe mused, it was not a happy thought.

"I am grateful that I did not, else I could never have been even this close to you, sweet Greta."

Margarethe frowned as she played the lively tune. "I care nothing for land or palaces. I want only to be with the man I love," she said, leaning close so Willem could catch her words above the music.

"But we knew this day would come. I am praying for strength when the time comes, but I fear I cannot bear to see you wed to another. By summer, I might have become a traveling minstrel or even a foot-soldier—anything to be away from here on your wedding day."

Margarethe nodded, not trusting her voice, and a tear slid down her face as Willem signaled the end of the song. He wiped the tear with his finger and anointed his own cheek with it, smiling sadly. "Do you remember the first time we spoke openly of our love?"

"Yes," she breathed. "We would not have spoken of it then, except I was so young and impetuous."

"I had wounded you," he admitted, tenderly caressing her hand, "though completely unintentionally. It will be two years come summer—that day when we rode out to our creek."

Margarethe remained silent, remembering.

"You did not mean it, but I, too, was hurt that day," he said. "In my heart I knew I loved you, though I had not confessed it. We sat side by side on the grass by the creek while you tossed daisies onto the surface of the water. Then you asked me, 'I want to know why you do not love me anymore.'"

"I'm sorry, Willem. I never meant to hurt you."

"I know. Nevertheless, the truth of your words stung like the tip of a lance. I had indeed been pushing you away. I could not permit you to continue your childish displays of affection for me. But I should have explained. I should not have turned my face from your kisses or held you away from me without a word. Still, I hoped you would understand."

"I understood only that the man I loved no longer loved me."

His laugh was brittle. "Ha! Nothing could have been further from the truth. I loved you from the day we met—sweet mischief and all. But as you blossomed from a child into a woman, I knew that I must put away all such thoughts of love. There would be no hope for us ever to marry."

Margarethe stormed to her feet and paced in front of the blazing fire in the grate. "It's all so unfair! That I should be forced to wed someone I *don't* love and be denied the one person in all the world I *do* love!"

When her fury subsided, Willem risked a comment. "I never told you, but I was tempted by your logic."

Hope renewed, she returned to her place beside him. "Were you?"

His eyes roamed her face as he reached for her hands. "I'm afraid so. . .until the next day, when we made up our rules."

"I never did agree to the no kissing rule," she maintained.

"How well I know, little one. But it was necessary. You

will be glad one day that you never kissed me."

"Ah, but I *have* kissed you."

"Not since you were no taller than a yearling fawn. And not since we each guessed the other's true feelings."

"Only because you won't let me!" She pursed her lips in a pout. "Tell me again why we may not kiss anymore."

Willem's usual explanation was accompanied by a playful grin. "Because once your lips have touched mine, you would be completely spoiled for anyone else's kisses forever."

"Oh, now I remember." She gave him a coy smile. "Sometimes I feel I should like to take a chance, though. Then at least I would have something pleasant to remember you by."

"Ah, *Liebchen,* we are not prophets that we can foretell what is to come. Perhaps there is still a chance for us." Margarethe searched his eyes, but they held no spark of promise. "Come, let's stand and stretch. We should practice the vocals before the hour's end."

She heaved another sigh and rose. "Could we stand near the window then? I want to see if our kitchen maid is still throwing snowballs."

Willem led the way to the window and opened the shutters, then tipped his head to one side as he studied the landscape. "Snowballs? You have not looked out lately. There is no snow."

Margarethe followed his gaze out over the bailey where the snow had melted and added its moisture to the mud and bourght traces of green to the soft bosom of the earth in the fields. With resignation, she looked again toward the gardens, where a few of the daffodils she had seen earlier, struggled to open to the meager sun.

Spring was surely on its way. She could do nothing to slow its arrival, nor the arrival of May Day—day her betrothal would be announced. The day two hearts would break.

two

Supper was a lavish affair. Following an oxtail soup flavored with leeks and garlic, the servants processed from the kitchens, bearing great platters of roasted pheasant nested in a bed of rice, wild boar with apples, and a rack of lamb. There were cheeses and breads and even exotic preserved foods from Spain.

Much to Margarethe's discomfort, Lord Otto and his four sons were seated at her table, along with Lord Einhard and Lady Mechthild. So there was to be no escape from boring conversation this night. It was all she could do to avoid casting glances in Willem's direction. As was the custom he, along with the other hirelings of the household, was seated at a lower table off to the side.

She made the best of the situation, chatting with her dinner companions, but welcomed the meal's finale—an elegant marzipan fashioned in the shape of a bear, the heraldic symbol of the House of Beroburg, in honor of their guest and his family. Now maybe they could get on with the musical entertainment, which—next to Willem—was her true passion in life.

His light touch on her shoulder sent a trail of tingles down her spine, and she rose to join him in front of the assembled guests, grateful for his rescue. They strummed a few chords, then began with some of the older songs, calling for the assembled crowd to join in on the chorus.

After a time, Willem whispered, "Are you ready to try the new piece, my lady?"

"As ready as I shall ever be," she assured him, willing away the queasy feeling in the pit of her stomach. What if they didn't find her melody pleasing?

He gave her a furtive wink and turned to address the hall. Margarethe was attending to the tuning of her lute, so missed his opening remarks until she heard him mention her name. "My lady wrote the song—both words and music. As her instructor, I could hardly allow such audacity," he paused to allow for a ripple of laughter, "so added an instrumental passage of my own. But for that single addition, this is the Lady Margarethe's own composition."

Willem's eyes twinkled as he glanced at her. She could hardly miss the fact that he was as handsome as ever—dressed as well as any of the lords in attendance, but in brighter colors. His parti-colored green and purple tunic reflected her own gown tonight, as he had requested. And even her aunt had entered into the preparations, persuading her to leave off her girlish cap and substitute instead a veil and circlet. The effect, she'd had to admit, was quite different from her everyday look. "Enchanting," Willem had murmured just before they'd taken the stage.

He nodded his readiness now, and she led out on the lute. It was always a joy to perform with him, but tonight it was as if they had been created to sing together, so flawlessly did their voices blend.

They sang the simple verses by turns, beginning with Margarethe:

> Cheerful did the sun shine, sparkling on the brook,
>> When my love came calling and on him I did look.
> In truth he was a fair one, wise and merry, too;
>> And if he never leaves me, then I'll believe him true.

The next lines suited Willem's elegant tenor:

> A lovely maid I saw there, tossing pebbles in the brook.

Her song was sweet, her beauty rare, as on her I did
   look.
Glad was I to go a'calling on the little country lass,
   For she is my dear wife now, 'til all my days shall pass.

They harmonized on the chorus:

'Til all our days shall pass,
   we'll be together all our days, together, you and me.
As ever on the brook flows down,
   constant to the sea.
As it's renewed by snow and rain,
   our love's fed from above.

Willem sang solo, "I always will be true to you."
And Margarethe answered, "You'll always be my love."

As the last notes faded, a shout went up in the vaulted hall.
But instead of an encore, Willem summoned some other
musicians to take their place and led Margarethe from the
platform. "Well done, my lady. Still, it's best not to overtire
your voice," he explained under his breath as he seated her.

She cocked her head. "I am not tired in the least, and we
are in fine voice tonight." There. She was sounding like a
petulant child, and he would be displeased.

"We shall let them call for us again. Meanwhile, you must
talk with your guests." His smile softened the edge of admonition in his voice.

Margarethe wrinkled her nose and glanced about her in dis-
taste. She was suspicious of the reason for Lord Otto's visit. It
was more than a report from the battlefront. Besides, Uncle
Einhard was not much interested in Otto's war, as he called it.
He much preferred to live in peace with their neighbors, and
hardly ever squabbled over a few furlongs of land. There was

quite enough to go around, it seemed to Margarethe.

Someone spoke, and she turned to see who had addressed her. It was Gregor, Lord Otto's third son, the least objectionable of the lot. He was rather attractive, but his nose and chin were both too big, which Margarethe reasoned kept him more humble than his brother Klaus, who could have been the model for the Roman statues in the castle chapel.

"Forgive me, Gregor. I did not catch what you were saying."

"I said that not only is Willem a fine musician, but he must be superior teacher."

She favored him with a smile. "I perceive a compliment intended for me as well."

"Your perception is right on the mark," he replied, his left cheek dimpling. He had a cleft chin, too, and Margarethe wondered how he ever managed to shave around such lumpiness.

"I am grateful to God that my uncle had the wisdom to hire him. My music means much to me and keeps me company when I am lonely for my family."

From her left, Klaus spoke up. "Your uncle has always had your best interests at heart, Margarethe. You'd be wise to remember that in the days to come."

She suppressed a shudder. Klaus would have been appealing were it not for his pompous manner. But she tried to remember her training, and concealed her irritation. "Thank you, Klaus." She turned again to Gregor. "When I was a child, you yourself were a good musician. Do you still make music?"

"I sing on occasion. . .but only for my own ears. I am not nearly so gifted as you, my lady."

"Do you play then?"

He held up his disfigured hands. "I have too long wielded the instruments of war, I fear."

Margarethe could not resist touching one jagged scar. "What a pity. Yet these hands and their skill with weapons of war have preserved your life."

Gregor's expression shifted subtly. "So you do care for this poor life of mine."

She was relieved when Klaus leaned over her to speak to his brother. "We are not being considerate of the entertainers," he said with a show of irritation. "Can't you keep still, Gregor, and listen to the song?"

Margarethe could not restrain a roll of her eyes for Gregor's benefit, and settled back in her chair to listen to the music, but not before Gregor covered her small hand with his much larger one.

❧

While Willem pretended to take in the performance of two musicians—one, playing a dulcimer, the other, a flute—he was really watching Margarethe sitting between the two sparring brothers. As for a prospective husband, Klaus would seem to be the more likely candidate. As Lord Otto's second son, he was in line to inherit, although it scarcely mattered. Lord Otto's wealth was a well-known fact, and there was plenty for all his sons, even Gottfried and young Albert.

Indeed, each son already held several estates and would likely have more if their father's victories continued. Only one major enemy remained before Otto would secure the valley with its roads linking Stuttgart with Zurich and Munich in the east with Strasbourg and the other great cities beyond. In fact, Lord Ewald's forces, weakened by years of war, might fall this very year.

If Margarethe were to be given her choice of the four unmarried brothers, whom would she choose? Even Albert was old enough to marry, and so she could take her pick. The subject was a sore point between them, and they had skirted the issue several times. But if Willem had to guess, he would say Margarethe might prefer Gregor. He was witty and kind and a fairly good singer.

Just then Margarethe caught Willem's eye, and he lifted his

chin in acknowledgment. He hoped that she would find happiness in the home of her husband—whoever that fortunate man turned out to be. Willem himself had been attending mass daily for the past few months, praying for Margarethe and her destiny.

Though she seldom attended mass, he knew she prayed, for he had caught her at it in the chapel and in her study chamber. He knew, too, that she insisted on reading the Scriptures for herself, asking Father Bernard to interpret difficult passages and asking all kinds of questions most people never thought to ask. But she had always been a curious child, and now that she was a woman, her bright mind still sought answers to the lofty themes of life.

Not long ago he had come upon Margarethe in prayer. When their lesson was concluded, he'd gently asked her about it, assuring her that he would understand if she chose not to share her private thoughts.

She surprised him by replying right away. "I was praying that I will be a good wife to. . .my future husband."

He nodded, a little sadly. "Then your prayers will be answered. As long as your relatives draw breath, you may be assured of having a husband."

She shook her head. "No. You don't understand. I pray for my future husband's safety and welfare, and that he will be blessed in every way. That he will love the Lord with all his heart, and I pray for. . .other things."

"Those are worthy prayers to be sure, my lady. I know that they will be heard. Dare I ask what 'other things' you might have mentioned to the Almighty?"

Eyes downcast, she went on. "It is something very important about my husband. Father Bernard has taught me that the Scriptures instruct us to ask for what we want and to keep on asking—like knocking on a door until is opened, or seeking some lost thing until it is found." She grew pensive, and he waited. "Oh, Willem, I hope you don't think me a foolish child."

"Never, Margarethe," he said. "Tell me what it is you ask for."

"I have asked God to give me you for a husband. I believe if He can do anything—anything at all—then even this request is not beyond Him. . ." With that, she broke down, sobbing pitifully and he felt his heart wrench. What she was asking was completely impossible.

"I love you so, little Greta. And I will join you in that prayer, no matter how hopeless it seems," he promised.

As soon as he had uttered the words, he regretted them. But a promise given was a promise he intended to honor, no matter what. . .

A sudden outburst from the dais brought Willem back to the present, in time to see Gregor capture Margarethe's hand. So. It was *this* son who would win her. That is, if God did not see fit to intervene. Willem might not be a warrior, only a simple musician. But he would storm the very gates of heaven with his petition for the love of his lady.

≥∙

Margarethe was most eager to see Willem this morning after their rousing success of the night before. Many people had told her how much they had enjoyed her song. Even Aunt Mechthild had seemed moved.

"You played and sang like an angel last night, my lady," Willem said when he joined her for their lesson. "Everyone is commending me as an exceptional instructor now."

Margarethe's joy was full. "They speak the truth."

"It is the student who makes the teacher proud," he said softly, lightly tracing her profile with one finger.

"We do sing and play well together, don't we?" She watched as he placed his lute on the table and turned back to her.

"That we do, my lady. Would that we could spend the rest of our lives discovering other things we do well together."

As naturally as breathing, Margarethe reached out as he drew steadily nearer, so close that she could see the little flecks of hazel in his eyes. "Kiss me, Willem. Please."

He swallowed and shook his head. "It would make matters worse, I fear." Despite his words, the next thing she knew, she was in his arms, hearing his whispered words, ragged with emotion. "I love you, my lady. I would die for you."

He had never held her this way before, and Margarethe scarcely moved, not wanting the moment to end. "I love you, too, Willem."

The moment was shattered by her uncle's stern voice from the doorway. "Margarethe. I will have a word with you."

They sprang apart, and Margarethe noticed the stricken look on Willem's face. She tried to still her own pounding heart and spoke as nearly normally as possible. "Yes, Uncle."

"I would speak with you, also, Willem. Later. Wait for me in my office chamber."

"Please, my lord. Lady Margarethe is innocent. I was pleased with her performance last night and was over-familiar in my congratulations, that's all."

Lord Einhard put up his hand. "In my office, please, Willem."

"Yes, my lord." Willem bowed stiffly and moved past him, glancing back at Margarethe, who ached for him and could give him no sign since her uncle was regarding her steadily.

"So, Margarethe," her uncle began the instant Willem was out the door, "is what I overheard true?"

"Yes, Uncle," she said, then shook her head in confusion. "That is—he was congratulating me, but I am not innocent. I offered the embrace."

Uncle Einhard's glassy-eyed stare was unreadable. "I also came to congratulate you. Your performance last night was superb. You have become a fine musician under that young man's instruction."

"Thank you, Uncle," Margarethe responded, her eyes stinging. What would her uncle do now? She shivered involuntarily as he walked up to her and cupped her chin in one hand, slowly tilting her head to look deep into her eyes.

"Do you love him, *Liebchen?*"

Margarethe took a deep breath. "Yes, Uncle, I do. I didn't mean to love him, for I know he can never be a husband to me. But he did nothing to encourage me. In fact, he. . ."

Uncle Einhard silenced her with an uplifted hand. "Greta, you are of an age to marry. I want you to be happy, as do Mechthild and your parents. You will have a say in the matter when the time comes. It is unfortunate that Willem cannot be considered as a prospect, for he is a man of honor and a nobleman. But he holds no land, and I cannot risk your future. Please understand."

"I do understand, Uncle. I only wish that things could be different."

After her uncle left, Margarethe looked out the window, wondering what would come to pass. She knew Willem's story would match hers, for he would simply tell the truth as she had done. They would not reveal the depth of their feelings for one another, but otherwise, they had nothing to hide.

From the day they had met when she was but a girl of eleven, Willem had always treated her as a lady, had ever been considerate of her. When she stumbled over her chords, he did not laugh. And when she needed correction for some childish infraction, he was gentle. He had listened to her dreams, and trusted her enough to share his dreams with her.

Margarethe wept softly as she thought of him now, facing her uncle alone in his chamber. What would Uncle Einhard do? He was a good man, a kind uncle to her, but he dealt with wrongdoers swiftly. And in the eyes of all those in authority—God and man alike—Willem was guilty.

three

Waiting anxiously in the lord's solar, Willem prayed that God would grant him favor with his employer. There was no question that he was guilty—of love, at least. Thus, deserving of punishment.

His foreboding eased somewhat, however, when Lord Einhard entered the solar and gestured for him to be seated. "I have just had a most interesting conversation with my niece."

The bearded man's gaze was unwavering, and Willem felt compelled to answer, his voice coming out in a croak. "Yes, my lord?"

"I came to her study chamber to offer the two of you my heartiest congratulations. With your. . .uh, dedication to my niece, Margarethe has surpassed all her family's hopes and expectations."

Willem shifted uneasily in his chair. "I thank you, my lord. But it was God who gave my lady the gift of music. I only helped her bring it to light." Feeling his master's intense scrutiny once more, he lowered his gaze to the rush-strewn floor.

"Up until now, you have been an asset to this household Willem," Lord Einhard continued. "But I fear that I have been selfish, keeping you on when you might have had a better opportunity elsewhere." Willem looked up, fully alert.

"I wanted to keep you on, partly because of Margarethe's affection for you, of course." Lord Einhard rose to warm his hands at the blazing fire in the hearth. "How *much* affection I have only just learned."

"Oh, my lord, if you knew how sorry—"

"Peace, Willem. Peace." The master turned his back to the warmth. In the morning light filtering through fashionably tinted windows and the flickering firelight, Lord Einhard looked fierce indeed—as daunting as the stag's head mounted on the stone wall above the mantel. Except for the compassion in his voice, Willem would have quite lost heart.

"I've called you in to tell you of an offer that has been tendered by Lord Otto of Beroburg Castle. He left before first light or he might be speaking for himself," Lord Einhard went on. "The position is an enviable one—that of chief musician. There would be no teaching duties—unless you desired them. However, Otto pays well, and he has a much larger household than I and entertains on a grander scale, so many more would benefit from your craft."

Willem already knew much about Beroburg. Situated on the trade route between Stuttgart and Zurich, the castle commanded the most strategic location of any manor house in the area. From its parapets, one could actually see across the entire valley. The speculation was that Lord Otto had been successful in his assaults because of the ability of his scouts to spy out the activities of neighboring enemies, giving him the advantage.

In any event, the castle was in the thick of things, and Lord Otto's household was an active one, going about the business of war during the spring and summer seasons—and hunting, harvesting crops planted by the peasants, and generally making merry the remainder of the year. It would be an ambitious move for Willem. If it were not for his love for Margarethe. . .

Still, to be near her each day—with no hope of wedding— was sweet agony. Surely both of them would be better off without his daily presence as a reminder of what could never be.

"Would I be leaving your household in a poor position should I move on, my lord?"

Lord Einhard seemed visibly relieved. "Not at all. It is a very good offer—for you and for Otto. As for me—" he turned back again to the fire— "I thought to make use of Margarethe's newly developed talent and offer her your old position. I should think it would amuse her."

And distract her from thoughts of me, Willem couldn't help thinking with a trace of bitterness. Still, that his remaining here might rob his dear one of such an opportunity was a shattering thought. "Greta deserves every chance," he murmured, then regretted slipping into the affectionate name he often used with her.

With Lord Einhard's back turned at the moment, Willem could not read his expression, but when he swung around, there was nothing to betray the fact that he might be disturbed. "Good. I'll send a messenger to Otto at once, letting him know your plans. In the meantime, you are relieved of your duties as Margarethe's music instructor, although I hope you understand that, under the circumstances—" he cleared his throat—" I am not charging you with any wrongdoing."

The man was a saint! And while Willem must leave his Greta, there was no help for it. "I am more than grateful, my lord."

And he was grateful. But there remained the task of breaking the news to his beloved.

❧

From the window of her bedchamber, Margarethe watched the messenger thundering across the drawbridge and wondered what important message he carried—and to whom. She listened to the carefree song of a bird building a nest in the belfry and wished with all her heart that she could take wings and fly above her pain. Then, hearing the sound of footsteps in the hallway, she hurried to see who it was.

Flinging the door wide, she found Willem, shoulders sagging, passing by. "Willem!" she called.

He pivoted on the spot where he stood, and she read his heart in his eyes.

"Tell me at once. What has happened?"

"I have been relieved of my duties at Adlerschloss and am to take up a new position at Beroburg."

The words fell like hammer blows. He seemed so remote, so distant. "Can't you tell me more? Have you been forbidden to talk with me?"

"It is not forbidden—" he let out a sigh— "merely unwise."

"Then come ride with me," she begged. "We could not get into any mischief on horseback."

A reluctant smile curved his lips, and she felt hope rising. "I suppose not. But I must notify your uncle, lest he think we're plotting to run away together."

"Now there's an idea—" She bit her lip, realizing the folly of it. "I'll get my riding wrap," she said quickly before he changed his mind.

She donned her favorite cloak, the purple one, lined in blue and trimmed with ermine, then ran down the stairs and out of the donjon. Willem was at the stable door ahead of her, saddling his horse, just as a groom led her mare up to be mounted.

They rode without speaking, past the castle walls and down the hill. Then they took the path off the road and into the forest. It was quiet here, lush with undergrowth, with only the sound of woodland creatures to disturb their thoughts. Here, too, the path widened between the massive conifers, allowing them to ride abreast.

The day was warmer than Margarethe had realized, a light breeze carrying the scent of evergreen and occasional whiffs of daffodil and narcissus growing at random in the moist earth. She scooped off her hood and turned to assess Willem's mood.

He was looking at her longingly, as if trying to memorize

her features, and the awful truth overwhelmed her with its finality. Willem was going away!

Her heart swelled with an ache too great to be borne, and she began to cry, gulping in great breaths of air.

Willem nudged his horse nearer hers. "I feel it, too, little one. Is there some way I can ease your grief?"

She glanced up through her tears and seized at the first thought that occurred to her. "You could run away with me. We could be traveling minstrels."

But he was shaking his head. "We wouldn't get far, *Liebchen*. You're this castle's greatest treasure, and you'll be needed now more than ever. Besides, we must be strong—do what is right, not what our hearts dictate."

His hand, holding the reins, was a white-knuckled fist. "What I would really like to do right now is to take you in my arms, but I promised your uncle—"

"*I* made no such promise!"

"Then come here, my lady." He scooted back on his steed and gathered her into the saddle in front of him, nestling her close. "This is madness, you know. If someone were to oversee us—"

"But no one is about. The battlefield is far away, and the farmers are all at their farming. And it isn't the hunting season, so we're quite safe here—and alone." She turned to gaze up into his eyes. "Are you still praying—about our condition, I mean?"

"Yes, sweet lady. I gave you my word, didn't I?"

Margarethe's horse moved off in search of a grassy sot beneath the trees, and Willem allowed his gelding to follow for a few paces. Then he released the reins and pulled Margarethe back against him.

"I do not want you to go, you know," she whispered.

"No. But you see how dangerous it is for us to be together. Only this morning, I held you for the first time, and now here we are again—" He broke off on a ragged breath. "I don't know how I will live without you."

"Beroburg is only an hour away. Perhaps we could meet—"

"No, Greta. After today, we must not allow ourselves to be alone again. You will be another man's wife, and I will not shame you or wrong him by taking such liberties."

Margarethe felt a surge of despair. "But we are both praying and maybe. . ."

"If our miracle happens, we will not be any the worse for staying apart, little one. But if God has other plans for us, then we will have nothing to repent of."

"Yes, Willem." She knew he spoke the truth. "I will not tempt you again. But when I visit Beroburg Castle in the future—and I shall—I hope you will speak to me there."

He chuckled—that deep, throaty sound she loved so much. "We will always be friends, sweet Margarethe, although after tomorrow, we will live in separate households."

"Tomorrow! It is too soon. I cannot let you go tomorrow." The tears that had been so near the surface, spilled over once more,and Willem held her until she quieted and dried her eyes, then kissed them.

"Greta, *Liebchen,* do not stop praying. And ask God to give me an extra measure of strength and wisdom."

She nodded miserably and tucked one of his light brown curls under his hood, a liripipe she had made for him. Though her needlework was poor at best, she had worked each stitch with loving care.

"It is time, my lady. Call your horse. We should be getting back to the castle."

"One kiss?" There was a pleading note in her voice.

Willem hesitated only a moment, succumbing to her plea. "Perhaps one small, very proper good-bye kiss. Can we manage that?"

Her answer was swift—both arms thrown about his neck,

her lips pressed to his in a gesture he thoroughly returned. Margarethe let her fingers linger on his face as she gazed at him, her wonder tinged with regret. "Now I know why you would never kiss me," she said. "It is true that no other lips will ever taste as sweet."

"Call your horse," he groaned in mock urgency. "We must get back."

Settled into her own saddle, Margarethe urged her horse to keep pace with Willem's, retracing their path through the forest as the shadows lengthened. By mutual and silent consent, they spoke only of pleasant things, sharing their memories of the day they had met.

"I don't recall what I was expecting when your aunt and uncle told me of the gifted child at Adlerschloss," Willem mused.

"And just what did they say?"

"That it was impossible for you to receive the musical training you deserved at home in the Schwarzwald, and so your parents fostered you to them in order for you to have the advantage of your aunt's talents."

"But she could not instruct me in the viel—"

"Yes—and so I was employed to fill that gap in your musical education." His eyes twinkled with the memory. "Now, of course, I understand why they called in another teacher. All your questions were exhausting them!"

Margarethe's laughter echoed across the forest floor, startling a squirrel, who darted into a tree. "I do not really ask so many questions, do I?"

A sudden sharp crack brought them to a halt along the trail. Willem inclined his head, listening. But there was no further sound and he continued.

"It must have been some forest animal. To get back to my story, I was not prepared for you. I had no notion what a gifted child looked like. And then you came in with mud-spattered clothing, your braids dragging the ground, and your hands behind your back. You curtsied politely when introduced, then told your aunt that you had found a new singer for the hall. 'He will fit right in,' you announced, then proceeded to plop a big, wet frog in her lap!"

"I really shouldn't have done that. Poor Aunt Mechthild. How she jumped!" Margarethe put her fingers to her lips to suppress a giggle. "But you never let me get away with such tricks, did you, Willem?"

"I learned to be wary when you hid your hands behind your back. Besides, your rascally grin usually gave you away." His expression grew sober. "If only you had grinned like that the first time you climbed into my lap, it might have forestalled all manner of trouble."

"Pah! There is nothing wrong with a child sitting on her teacher's lap."

"True. But the child has become a woman," he reminded her.

They rode in silence for the remainder of the way. And when the castle came into view, they kept their mounts at a discreet distance.

⁂

Lord Einhard called on the jugglers instead of the musicians that evening at dinner, and Willem was grateful for the reprieve. With his departure so near at hand, singing with Margarethe again would have been sheer torture. The jugglers, too, were happy with the decision, since they normally worked in the kitchen and were eager to escape their chores.

Willem had fared well in this house, never having had any duty but that of singer and musical tutor, teaching Margarethe and a few others from time to time. He was highly esteemed and had been given his own chamber, like a member of the family. Therefore, his guilt was all the heavier this night, knowing that he had dishonored his lord and his lady by falling in love with their niece.

Worse still, he had done little to rebuff Margarethe's adoration. With her tender, young heart, he should have taken sterner measures to keep their relationship purely platonic. But in spite of all that, Lord Einhard had not dismissed him in disgrace, and had even allowed him to accept another position. Surely the love of God was manifest here. Willem must thank the good Lord for His favor and repent of bringing trouble to this household.

❧

Early in the morning, before dawn, Willem arose, packed his few personal belongings, and prepared to attend morning Mass in the chapel. Later he would load a borrowed pack horse, being careful of his instruments, and set out for Beroburg. But first, there was a pressing matter to attend to.

In the chapel, Willem prayed fervently, unmindful of anyone around him, so eager was he to set his heart right with God. When at last he looked about him, he was surprised to find Margarethe there. But she kept her hood over her face, as if she did not want to be recognized, and slipped out before any of the others.

After Mass, Father Bernard approached him and spoke warmly, offering a benediction: *"Dominus vultum suum ad vos et det vobis pacem,"* he said. "May the Lord show His face to you and give you peace."

Willem thanked the priest and added that blessing to the prayers he prayed for Margarethe.

She was breaking her fast in the great hall alone at a trestle table when he arrived. He slid in beside her and tore off a chunk of bread from the loaf in front of them.

"Did you speak with Father Bernard?" she asked.

"Briefly. He had a blessing for me."

"Good. God will go with you. But I wanted to help, too, so I brought you some cheese." There was a goatskin of wine and a brick of hard cheese, along with another loaf of the flaky bread. "Oh, do be careful! The road is dangerous this time of year. I've heard there are robbers and—"

"Shh." He covered her lips with his fingers. "Where is your faith, little one? I must hurry now before the family comes in. It wouldn't do for them to think I was making things difficult for you by delaying."

"Oh, Willem, there is so little time. And to think that, as a fosterling, I could have dined with you everyday for the past five years instead of at the lord's table. And now it is too late," she moaned. "Tonight you will sit at meat in Lord Otto's house."

He nodded. "We may well think of other things we could have done differently over the next few days." *And months and years,* he added mentally. "But let us remember the good things only. I pray you will be diligent with your music— remember the things I have taught you. Will you sing from your belly instead of your throat? And will you keep your youngest finger handy at all times when you are playing viel, instead of curling it up out of the way?"

"Yes, teacher." She laughed—a tinkling sound that echoed like the smallest handbell. "Some things I will never forget."

"Nor will I, sweet lady. Nor will I."

four

Margarethe was grateful for Father Bernard's patience at morning studies. A fortunate thing, since she found herself calling upon it over and over again during her Latin and geometry lessons. When she immersed herself in history, asking many questions, the hour flew. But when it was over, she remembered that it was time for music, and that she had no teacher.

"You will miss Willem, will you not, my child?" Father Bernard asked gently.

"You have read my heart, Father."

He chuckled. "It is your *face* I have read."

"I am used to having him around, and—"

"And you love him."

Margarethe cast the old priest a sharp glance. "Did he speak with you. . .about me?"

"There was no need. I knew. I cannot take his place, of course, but perhaps you and I could share some music from time to time."

She nodded, the idea holding much appeal. "I would like that." Father's singing voice was as rusty as an old coat of mail, but he handled wind instruments admirably.

He looked a little shy just now, a novel thing. "I'm free at the moment, as a matter of fact, having no more duties until after dinner."

Margarethe jumped up. "Which instrument do you prefer? I'll fetch it."

"A doucaine, please. I should think sackbut and lute would make an interesting duet."

Despite her longings for Willem, Margarethe was intrigued. "Then you must have a song in mind." She handed him his instrument and took up her lute.

" 'The Lady in Blue.' I will lead out, then. . .well, we'll see."

"I know that song. It's one of Aunt Mechthild's favorites." Margarethe tuned her lute, then nodded for Father to begin.

They were well into the chorus when she heard her aunt's rich mezzo-soprano behind her. Father Bernard switched to a harmony part immediately, evidence that he had seen his lady coming.

At the end of the song, Margarethe put down her lute and hugged her aunt. "I'm so glad you joined our ensemble. What shall we play now?"

"How about 'The Wood Clothed in Daffodils'?"

The bittersweet song was not so pleasing since it reminded Margarethe that time was marching relentlessly toward May Day. At the song's conclusion, and without consulting the others, she struck the beginning chords of *"Dominus Vobiscum."* Lady Mechthild followed on her recorder.

Once the tune was underway, Margarethe slipped out of the chamber and into the music room, where she picked up a viel, checked the tuning, then reentered the room, playing in harmony with the other instruments.

The combination with this modal piece was haunting, and as the final notes trailed away, the three of them sat in silence, sensing the sacredness of the moment. Remembering that these were the last words she had uttered to Willem before he took his leave, Margarethe felt the sting of tears behind her eyes. *"Dominus vobiscum*—God go with you."

Inspired, she took up her viel again and began to play, her fingers flowing with the mood of the moment. The others listened and when she repeated the melody, Lady Mechthild joined in.

Father Bernard laid aside his doucaine and reached for some parchment and a quill pen. "This one deserves marking down for the future," he observed. "We must play it again."

He left them then to prepare for the midday meal, and Margarethe laughed in delight. "What a pleasant morning, after all, Aunt. I had forgotten how well we make music together."

"Then we shall do it often. But now you are the teacher, and I, the student. I must learn how to make a viel sing as you do. The naughty instrument does not behave as well for me."

Margarethe smiled, recalling Willem's admonition. She had followed his advice, curling her smallest finger just so, and it had helped. Perhaps she *could* teach her aunt a thing or two. The notion buoyed her spirits considerably. But it did not remove the ache from her heart when she thought of her lost love.

❧

A thousand little memories plagued Margarethe during the long afternoon. Willem—dining with the other retainers at his trestle table at the noon hour. Willem—astride a stallion, looking as proud as any lord. Willem—tears sparking his blue eyes at their parting. . .

Feeling restless, she could not keep her mind on her dreaded needlework. She left the tapestry frame and went to the window overlooking the bailey. There was the little kitchen maid, throwing out a pail of water. The smithy was shoeing a horse. And from here, she could see peasants in the fields—pruning the grapevines. Everyone, it seemed, was busy, doing some useful work. Only she was left with nothing to do.

Leaving the room, she found Lady Mechthild teaching her youngest child, Friedrich, in the solar. He was seven now and would soon be fostered to another household to further his education. He would begin as a page, like other boys his age, then go on to be trained as a knight, as befitted his station in life.

Her thoughts, apparently with a mind of their own, strayed again to Willem. But only for an instant as she willed her heart to obey. "Would Uncle Einhard be needing some help with the accounts?"

"Why not ask, my dear? He's in the next chamber." The woman turned again to answer some childish question about the story she was reading to her little son.

At the door of her uncle's office chamber, Margarethe waited until he glanced up from his papers. "Oh, so there you are," he said at last. "Is something wrong?"

"No, Uncle. Nothing. I was bored and thought I might be of some help to you. I have been practicing my letters with Father Bernard and—"

Her uncle's grave expression halted her words. "Come here, Greta." She approached and took a seat cushioned in velvet. "I was just reading some of the proposals offered by your many suitors."

"Then I'm sorry I intruded. I'd rather not think of such things today." She rose and was about to leave when her uncle gestured for her to remain.

"I realize the timing is poor. But you are of age now, and we can no longer put off your betrothal, or your suitors shall all grow tired of waiting. One of them has long since given up and withdrawn his offer."

She was curious in spite of herself. "Which one?"

"Ludwig von Beroburg—the eldest son."

"Oh. He would have been a valuable ally for you. But he is Aunt's nephew, so you will still be joined."

"True. Still, these propositions have been coming since you were twelve. And now that you are a woman of substantial grace and beauty—" he regarded her once again— "not to mention your exceptional talents, it seems the list has only grown longer."

She had to smile. "And will you truly allow me to choose my husband, Uncle?"

"I said you would have a say in it. But I have narrowed your choices to these six." He indicated the stack of parchments on his table. "I would not want to overlook anyone who might be worthy to claim your hand."

"And have you a preference?"

It was clear that her uncle was loathe to answer. "I want you to be happy, child. At the same time, I must take into account what is best for our household. These are turbulent times. We have lost revenue in the fields due to the floods. Then this everlasting war of Otto's has involved us more than I would like." He rose to pace before the fire, hands behind his back. It was as if she were not even in the room. "Still, it might be wise to strengthen our ties with the House of Otto. I have not supported him in battle as often as he might have wished, being reluctant to lose any of my own men for a cause so far removed from my borders."

He paced some more, and Margarethe waited, fascinated with his monologue, so revealing of the affairs of this family. "Of course, having our daughter Jolan there these past two years has helped, though she can form no lasting alliance since she is too closely related to marry any of Otto's sons."

At this, Margarethe spoke up, unable to contain her disgust. "Uncle Otto is the only person I know who is so fussy about cousins marrying. He's certainly not strict about other things forbidden by the Church!"

At this, Uncle Einhard let out a loud burst of laughter. "Aha! It seems I do recall being served meat there during Lent once—and finding it quite enjoyable, too." He straightened his face. "But Jolan is reconciled to having Albert as nothing more than a cousin, and besides that, we were speaking of your prospects, I believe. As you know, any of Otto's four sons would be an excellent match."

She supposed there was no hope for it, but perhaps she could put off the decision just a little longer. "Will Jolan marry soon? She is only two years younger than I."

Uncle Einhard returned to his chair and narrowed his gaze to look directly into her eyes. Margarethe knew that he suspected this delaying tactic, but he answered kindly. "It won't be long before she has her choice of suitors as well."

"Then I would like to allow her to consider Selig and Helmhold, along with the others. As for me, I shall choose one of Otto's sons, Uncle, for I know it would please you."

Uncle Einhard's gaze softened. "Good. Very good, Greta. I had hoped you would come to that decision on your own. Do you have a particular son in mind?"

She sighed, thinking again of Willem and wishing it could be *their* betrothal under discussion. "Yes," she conceded weakly. "Of those four, I would choose Gregor, I suppose."

Now that she had been so bold, she regretted it at once. "Still, I really don't know him very well. Perhaps I should speak with Jolan about him. Living in the same household, she would know. He could be foul-tempered or stingy or a boor, for that matter."

Uncle Einhard seemed amused, but consented readily enough. "You're right to consider carefully. Besides, it is time Jolan came home for a visit. So I shall send for her. In the meantime, I'll tell Mechthild that you have agreed to marry one of her nephews—though I'll be sure not to mention which one. It shall be our secret."

He rose in dismissal and Margarethe followed suit, releasing a long sigh. Her uncle's attempt at humor had failed miserably. Instead of bringing a smile, Margarethe felt her cheeks growing moist with tears.

"Greta, dear child, I love you as my own daughter. I know

how hard this must be for you. But all will be well, you'll see."

"I do hope you're right, Uncle. It will take me a while to get used to—"

"I know, *Liebchen*. I know." He held out his arms, and she walked into them, sobbing openly. How many tears had she shed in these past few days? If this continued, she would not have to worry about marrying. No man would want a wife with red eyes and a voice as raspy and shrill as a shrew.

❧

When Willem arrived at Beroburg, he was greeted warmly by Lord Otto's wife, Lady Edeltraud. "Otto will be sorry to have missed your arrival," she said. "But he was called to the battlefield. Would you like to get settled before we talk?"

Willem bowed over her hand. "I am entirely at your disposal, my lady. My journey was not overlong; therefore, I'm not tired. But I would like to rid myself of some of this mud." He swiped at his mud-spattered cloak.

"Refresh yourself then. We'll talk later." She summoned a page, a fresh-faced lad of about ten, who appeared instantly to show Willem to his quarters and help with this belongings. But the sack of musical instruments he carried himself.

He found his bedchamber slightly smaller than the one he had occupied at Adlerschloss. With the addition of an anteroom, however, furnished with a table and chair, the walls hung in rich tapestries, his accommodations were even more sumptuous. Indeed, this castle was quite large, having been added onto through the years, including garderobes, for which Willem was most grateful. Other options for taking care of personal needs were either inconvenient or downright crude.

Willem thanked the page and stowed his possessions in a coffer. Then after washing his face and hands in a bowl of water prepared for him, he joined Lady Edeltraud in the solar.

She was eager to get on with the discussion of his duties, mentioning a handsome wage.

"And if that is not enough," she said, scanning his face anxiously, "Otto has authorized me to offer more—with an additional stipend for instructing our musicians and fosterlings, if you are so inclined."

He nodded thoughtfully. "You are generous, my lady. When can I meet with the other musicians?"

The lady sighed. Though she seemed physically robust— tall and broad-shouldered—the constant warfare of past years had surely taken a toll of her spirits. "I'm afraid there are only a few—some women and two men. All the others are with Otto in battle. It has not been going well this week."

"I will pray them Godspeed," Willem murmured, his stomach twisting at the thought that he might be similarly pressed into service one day.

Lady Edeltraud waved a hand. "You need not concern yourself. We've become accustomed to this way of life. Now, is there anything else we can do to make your stay with us more pleasant?"

"Well, there is the matter of a borrowed horse. I could return it on the Lord's Day if you cannot spare me on a working day."

The lady appeared to be thinking. "Not even those barbarians Otto fights will do battle on the Lord's Day, so the men will be home. Music would encourage them. I pray you might be willing to play for them then, or do you object to working on that day?"

Willem inclined his head and replied solemnly, "To serve you is to serve Him, my lady."

❧

On his way into the banquet hall, Willem was hailed by a young woman. To his delight, he saw that it was Jolan, striding briskly toward him.

"It really is you, Willem. Then have you finally given your consent to join this household?"

"I have. I might say that you're looking well, my lady." Like his Greta, the young girl had blossomed into a lovely young woman—though she was more like her father in appearance than her mother or her sweet cousin.

"How will Greta manage without her handsome teacher?"

"Ah. . ." To his utter embarrassment, nothing came to mind, and he felt a slow flush heat his cheeks.

"Never mind. Her loss is my gain, for we've been in need of a music instructor. My high notes—when I move from chest voice to head voice—are most unpredictable lately."

He suspected he knew the cause of the symptoms she was describing, but restrained the grin that threatened to break across his face. At a certain stage in life, young lads had much the same problem. Her vocal problem was surely related to her age and would settle on its own. "It would be my pleasure to assist you."

"We have all been hoping that you would decide to come here. We've been too long without a voice teacher and someone to help us make merry in these dismal halls. But couldn't you have come sooner? The trip is not so very long except when it is raining or snowing."

"And, of course—" he went along with her jest— "it never rains or snows in Bavaria."

"Of course not!" Her rosy cheeks dimpled. "You'll do us all good, Willem." She glanced at the lord's table. "I had better go. Lady Edeltraud is scowling at me. Well met, Willem. Let me know when you will have time to help my poor voice."

"It is no small gift you have, my lady," Willem protested. "We shall meet again."

He watched her swift departure as he seated himself, then bowed for prayer before the meal. Jolan did look well, and she had matured considerably since she had been his student at Adlerschloss. Such a voice she had, and now that it had deepened a bit, he could work with it. Her sense of pitch was slightly lacking, but she had the resonant range of her mother, Lady Mechthild. He welcomed the challenge.

As the servitors brought in the food, Willem noticed that most of them were women. So it was true that Lord Otto had pressed nearly every available man into service. If this continued, it wouldn't be long before the lord of the castle would be calling on his neighbors at Adlerschloss for reinforcements. Thinking of the home he had just left—and Margarethe—brought a fresh pang of grief.

He was relieved when Lady Edeltraud called him forward to be introduced to the household. "Our new chief musician has agreed to favor us with a song," she said. "Come now, Willem. But please—give us anything but a battle song!"

five

The next day in the morning hours, Willem auditioned the musicians one by one, then assembled them as a group to rehearse for the evening's entertainment. In the process, he noted individual strengths and weaknesses, hoping to give encouragement where it was needed. There seemed to be a dearth of enthusiasm about the place—a general malaise hanging over the entire castle. He wasn't sure it was the war only that robbed these good folk of their life and vitality.

Shrugging off the effects of melancholy, lest it settle over him, he set off to find the chapel. At this hour, it would be deserted. All the better. He needed time to pray. For his new household. For the wisdom and discernment to know how to help them. And, of course, for Margarethe and her impossible dream.

Afterward, he strolled in the bailey, dropping by the stables to see to his horse and the pack animal he had borrowed from Lord Einhard. They had been fed and watered and were nibbling at the straw in the stall. He talked with the groom and the avener for a while, then went out again, noticing a commotion at the gate.

No one had expected the soldiers home that night, but it appeared that there had been a lull in the fighting, and Lord Otto, his sons, and many of his men arrived an hour before sunset.

Suddenly there were people everywhere. Knights in bloodstained armor. Squires stabling the horses, lathered from a hard ride. A flurry of maids and pages hurrying to lay out fresh linens for the baths, and extra cups and trenchers in the

42

banquet hall. And Lady Edeltraud, quietly supervising—instructing the steward to prepare several additional courses for the meal, then calling for the physician and other healers—including Lady Jolan—to help tend the wounded.

Ever practical, she arranged for a portion of the great hall to be curtained off as a bathing area and hospital. And soon there was a steady procession of servants bringing steaming cauldrons of water, strips of bandaging, and various medicinal herbs from the garden.

Willem wondered how he could help, and remembered his prayer not an hour past. This would be his chance to offer encouragement. Music was as healing—to his mind, at least—as any herb, and he went in search of the other musicians to tell them of his plan and enlist their aid.

He was talking with some of them when he heard a manly voice call out, and turned to find Gregor striding toward him. "Lord Gregor! How good to see that you escaped an enemy arrow or spear," he said as they clasped arms in greeting.

"I am well," Gregor announced. "Are you here for a visit, or has my father finally persuaded you to join this household?"

Willem grinned. "I'm here to stay—as long as I can be of service. And you and the other fighting men—what about you?"

"It depends on word from our scouts. We may be here for the night only, or we may rest another day. But it's good to be home, and to have you here." He glanced around to make sure the other musicians had left, then added, "We can use some pleasant music in this drafty old hall. I've been longing to lend my voice to some harmonies, but have had no inspiration until now."

Gregor looked so comically sad that Willem laughed. "You shall sing with us tonight. No doubt this group will want many songs."

A page appeared at Gregor's elbow. "Your bath is ready, my lord."

"Ah, and not a moment too soon. A hot bath is sorely needed about now. As for this evening's songs, Willem, I would suggest that long ballad you wrote about the victorious lord—"

"I've had my instructions from Lady Edeltraud. No battle songs. . .allowed at dinner yesterday."

"So my mother has already made use of your talents." He nodded. "But we are here now, and the men need uplifting. We've suffered defeat lately on the field. Come, sit with me while I bathe, and I'll tell you about our latest skirmish."

Willem followed Gregor into the curtained-off partition, hoping the others would not find his presence offensive. Perhaps they would even be amused.

Inside, Willem dropped down onto a bench that ran alongside the wall while Gregor disrobed with the help of a page. Others stood about in various stages of dress—some being assisted out of their heavy mail and into one of four large wooden tubs filled with soapy water. One such tub stood waiting for Gregor.

He settled into the suds with a loud sigh and closed his eyes. "With this bath and a night's sleep, I may be fit for battle again come morning."

Willem launched into a rousing verse of a tune Gregor was likely to know. It wasn't long before the young lord was singing along, blending his voice in harmony.

When they were done, one of the other men—a knight judging from his age and scars—spoke up. "My lord, what I have heard about Willem is true. He can sing with anyone, and make them sound good."

A hearty chorus of laughter rang out through the hall. This time, when Willem struck up a tune, the others joined in lustily. A good quarter of an hour went by before a page entered to wash backs. When there was a lull in the music, he was quick to take advantage. "Pardon me, my lord, but Lady Edeltraud told me to ask all of you to bathe faster. The supper is cooling."

Gregor frowned. "You may tell my mother that I am not done with singing yet, and that I will leave my bath when the songs are through!" he bellowed, obviously pitching his voice so his lady mother would hear.

"My lord, I love my life," said the little fellow, "and do not wish to cross my lady."

Gregor chuckled. "Wise lad—to know, at such a young and tender age, whose wrath to fear!"

❧

There was no music at Adlerschloss the night Willem left. Instead, Lord Einhard called for the games to be brought out after supper. Margarethe liked chess well enough and would have challenged Lady Mechthild, but she was occupied in some kind of child's play with young Friedrich.

When she realized that Lord Einhard had excused himself to attend to some business and that Father Bernard was also nowhere to be seen, she approached the youngest knight, who was sitting by himself at one of the trestle tables, his bandaged ankle propped on a stool.

He appeared alarmed when he saw her with her game board and her leather bag of chessman, and glanced about the hall nervously, as if seeking escape.

"Greetings, Sir Johan," she began. "Will you be my opponent tonight?"

"Uh . .with pleasure, my lady. But I hope you don't mind a short game."

She gave him a curious look. "And just what do you mean by that?"

"I am quite good at chess."

She laid the board on the table between them and got out

her playing pieces. "Then mind your moves. It wouldn't be wise to let down your guard just because I am a lady."

‌ 𝕒

Willem had difficulty falling asleep. It had been Lord Otto himself who had briefed him on the progress of the war, inviting him to the solar while he gave the news to Lady Edeltraud, Jolan, and the rest of the family at home. It was clear that Otto was concerned that he might have failed to consider his enemy's superior strength—now that he had obtained replacements and supplies from some unknown source. To regroup, therefore, Otto had broken off the battle at the first opportunity, and had fallen back. In the meantime, he would wait for the reports of his scouts, who had set up a relay system to forward messages to their general.

With Albert's castle in jeopardy, Otto had dispatched his youngest son there with what he hoped would be an adequate armed guard and a unit of archers. It was not likely that the nearby villagers would be threatened, but they should take no chances.

"I have no idea where Ewald has gotten his extra support," Otto fumed. "He can hardly afford mercenaries, so I fear that one of our neighbors may have reconsidered his alliance with me. If that's the case, we may be facing war on two fronts."

His audience was stone silent as he paced in front of the fire. At length, he looked up, searching the faces until his gaze fell on Willem, and his countenance brightened. "Ah, there's a good man. It is you, Willem, who have fortified us today with your songs and your merrymaking. I was questioning the wisdom of falling back until I realized that the men were receiving far more than a few hours' rest and a hot meal. They've received hope—from your music. Already you are proving to be an asset to this house." He squinted at Willem. "What is it, my good man? You appear disturbed. Is Edeltraud paying you well enough?"

"It's not that, my lord. I was just wondering if you would call for troops from among your allies?"

Otto sighed and resumed his pacing. "This is really my battle. But I could use some help. Still, it's a complicated situation. I would hate to risk my friends' good will. . ." He seemed to be mulling over the idea, but offered no further enlightenment.

"Forgive my inquisitiveness, my lord," Willem murmured, fearing he had overstepped.

"Nonsense. As a new member of this household, you have every right to know what is going on under this roof and abroad."

Sleep was elusive when Willem was ready to retire for the night. His thoughts roiled as he considered just what Lord Otto might do. He knew the cause—protecting his family and their possessions—was just, and Willem had no qualms about lending his support. But Lord Einhard should be advised.

Still sleepless, Willem arose, lit a candle, and wrote a letter to his former employer. While Willem owed his new master his loyalty, he could not put aside his years as chief musician of Adlerschloss. And there was more. He would not desert the one he loved more than he loved himself—Margarethe. If Lord Otto's army lost the war, her life might be at risk as well.

❧

Albert roamed the battlements of the castle, scanning the countryside for signs of activity. Even at twenty, he was strategist enough to know that movement of troops at night would spell trouble. Indeed, every male in his father's household knew, by the time he was a lad of eight, that an ominous silence could well signal the eve of battle.

At midnight, a scout rode in with the news that a large battalion of foot soldiers was moving in their direction from the southwest. Albert called for his squire and a messenger, the first link in the relay system. "Tell Lord Otto that he is to come at once. We may not have much time before we are under siege."

He whirled to summon a page. "You, boy! Rouse the knights and the other fighting men and tell them it is full armor. But before you do, bring me the captain of the guard. I need a word with him."

"Yes, my lord." The lad bowed and flew to do his bidding.

Sir Jakob was not long in coming. "You called for me, my lord?"

Albert nodded. "Choose the most convincing of your men and send them into the village. Have them wake the people and bid them come within the castle walls at once. They will find sanctuary here."

Such was not the case only two years past, when his father had first invaded this small pocket of civilization, Albert knew. Fearing the lord of the manor more than the approaching enemy, the villagers had refused to take asylum in the castle. Instead, they had faced Lord Otto and his men, confident that their lives could be no worse off with this invader.

In truth, the "barbarian" invader had proven to be a benevolent ruler. Otto had built them a church, lowered their taxes, and otherwise looked out for them in the face of growing political unrest. Not only that, but hadn't his father appointed Albert himself to manage castle affairs, including protecting the people from their enemies—whoever those enemies might happen to be?

He could only pray that they would listen to the knights he had dispatched to warn them. He could only pray. . .

❧

Leaving her bed sometime in the night, Margarethe fell on her knees, reasoning that if she were to be sleepless, she might just as well put the time to good use. As it was, there were plenty of targets for her prayers.

She began with the one dearest to her heart. "Willem—"

The very mention of his name sent a shaft of pain deep into her heart. "If I should not love him, Father, then change my mind and fill my thoughts with more useful things. I know Lord Otto has other plans for me, but I cannot imagine finding a better husband. Not in all of Bavaria!"

She thought of her loneliness and prayed that her uncle would send quickly for Jolan. It would do her good to have another young woman about—someone she could trust with her dreams of Willem. Still, she must guard her tongue, lest she speak too much of him and betray her heart.

She prayed silently for a few minutes more, until she realized that her prayers had all been selfish ones, directed toward her own sad state. She must remedy that at once, and so she addressed the matter of others—her aunt and uncle, the cousins, Father Bernard—

Margarethe was unaware that she had been nodding until she awoke from a startling dream. She had seen Albert, riding horseback through a village, crying out in despair! Strewn about like so much litter were dead bodies, and smoke drifted about from sacking fires.

For a moment she was embarrassed to realize that she had fallen asleep at her prayers, then wondered if it was God who had sent the dream. Then, fully alert, she gave herself to a frenzied barrage of prayer-like arrows aimed into the darkness, not knowing where they would land. Only God knew. She prayed her aim was true.

❧

Willem was surprised to see Lord Einhard's messenger, who arrived while the household was still at table breaking their fast. The message must be extremely important, and reminded him that he had an urgent message to send.

"Stay, Sir Messenger," said Lady Jolan when the young man handed her the scroll, "while I read this to see if a return reply is expected."

Recognizing the lad, Willem smiled as he walked up. "Greetings. Any luck with that serving maid yet?" he whispered behind his hand.

"Uh. . .yes," said the boy, glancing at the lady, who was absorbed in her letter. "In fact, we are going to take a walk today," he whispered back.

Relieved that he would have swift transit for his message, Willem smiled. "Then you are going back right away! You can take a letter for Lord Einhard."

"Indeed, I would go with you now," said Jolan, showing her dimple, "had I not been promised a voice lesson first." She looked especially beguiling when she pursed her lips in that way, Willem thought, wondering how such a thought had come to him with Margarethe constantly on his mind.

The messenger, it appeared, was in no hurry to be gone—despite his plans for an outing with the scullery maid. "I must let the horse rest. I'm afraid I rode him too hard on the way here."

"Then let him rest and ride the horse I borrowed. He needs to be returned to Lord Einhard anyway."

Willem walked out with the messenger and stopped off at the stables to wish the lad Godspeed and send him on his way. He was appalled to see the condition of the horse the messenger had ridden in.

"How would you like to run so far with a great beast on your back?"

The lad had the grace to blush. "I wouldn't like it at all. And the groom has already abused me on this same point."

"He's a good man then." Willem nodded. "Now be off with you. And treat this animal better. Ride and walk alternately on your return trip."

Willem watched the messenger mount up and begin his journey home to Adlerschloss. Immediately the vision of the familiar halls beckoned. How he wished he could be making that trip right now—back to Margarethe.

અ

By mid-morning, Albert was dismayed at the turnout. Only a handful of villagers had answered his summons and shown up here at the castle. But he greeted them all courteously. "Why didn't the others come?" he asked one old man, who had shuffled over to stand by the fire.

"Because they were all warm in their beds and felt no need. They have forgotten the former invaders before you. Begging your pardon, your lordship, but they too safe now to bother leaving their homes."

Albert was truly concerned now. "Good sir, would you ride back into the village with my knights and speak to your people? I fear for their lives."

"I will go if you require it, my lord."

"I do not require it. I merely ask it."

The old man nodded. "Then I will go."

Albert arranged for a good horse and a sturdy cloak for the man and sent him out with instructions to the knights who accompanied him. "Take care now. And bring him back with you—along with all the others you can persuade. I think I see the glint of armor in the morning sun."

An hour later, when the knights returned, there was still only a trickle of peasants coming in from the countryside. And when the last of his soldiers, including the old man, were safely within the walls, Albert reluctantly secured the gates and posted archers on the walls.

six

Lord Einhard took Willem's letter into the solar to read as soon as it arrived.

He found Lady Mechthild there, working on her tapestry—an intricate design of flowers and leaves bordering a forest scene. "What is it?" she asked, looking up from her loom.

"Willem writes to tell me of the situation at Beroburg. I did not know the war had taken such a turn. He says Otto will not ask his allies for troops but may hire mercenaries instead."

Mechthild appeared puzzled. "He hates that practice. Why would he do such a thing?"

He handed over the letter so she could read it for herself. "It sounds quite serious," she observed, clearly alarmed.

"I am stricken with guilt that he would not call on me for help." He rose to pace restlessly, then turned to regard his wife. "Would Otto take offense if I sent troops without consulting him?"

She cocked her head and gently posed a question. "Would you do it out of a guilty conscience, or because my brother truly needs your help?"

He shook his head. "It is this letter, Mechthild. Willem has always had keen discernment. If he senses that Otto's army is depressed, then I believe it. A few extra men might lend encouragement. Besides, hiring mercenaries could take weeks. Ewald might hit Otto hard before a new contingent of forces could be ready to fight."

Einhard stood and gazed out the window at the soldiers drilling in the field below. "I will put it to the men."

❧

The attack—a flurry of arrows launched over the castle walls—came just before dawn while Mass was being said. Tower guards also reported enemy activity in the nearby village. It was a minor siege, broken off after scarcely an hour, thanks to Albert's well-executed defense. There was only one casualty—an archer on the wall, who took a crossbow bolt in the neck.

Unfortunately, the unprotected villagers had not fared as well, he feared. To assess the damage, Albert mounted the turret and looked out over the valley. It appeared that the enemy had withdrawn, but the source of the heavy smoke was surely other than random cooking fires, built by the peasants as they went about the business of preparing their morning meal.

"We suspect there might be soldiers still in the village, my lord," the lookout said.

At that, Albert felt a wave of disgust, confident he knew what the marauders were up to. "Any sign that the main body of the army is simply feinting?"

"No, my lord. From what I could see, the main force has withdrawn."

"Then keep a sharp eye until relieved and report any further activity." He waved the young man away and descended the stairs to the bailey to learn the latest from his scouts who had ridden in.

The enemy troops seemed to have pulled back, at least for the moment, but Otto's men, who had been alerted as to the problem at Engelburg and should have set out by now to reinforce the castle guard, had not yet been spotted. It was not a good omen.

Albert summoned his men, and they gathered in the early morning sunlight, plumed helmets gleaming, shields reflecting the morning sun. It was a small, but formidable-looking battalion, and their mounts shifted restlessly beneath them as they awaited orders from their commander.

"We must ride into the village at once. Bring back—alive—any soldiers you find loitering behind. I must learn today where Ewald has drawn his extra troops."

Albert then called for his squire to bring his war horse. "My lord, surely you would not risk your own life on such a mission," the squire objected.

Albert donned his helmet and swung into the saddle. "These are my people, and it is my duty to protect them. You there, Sir Jakob, half the foot soldiers will remain here with you to guard the castle. The remainder will follow me. Forward!"

With that, he moved out in front and, taking the lead, clattered across the drawbridge, down the rutted road, and toward the village at full gallop.

To his horror, the first sight to greet him was the bodies of two small children, sprawled lifelessly along the road. "See to a proper burial for these little ones," he ordered a couple of his knights. "In the churchyard yonder."

Then noticing the destruction of a portion of the church he had ordered built, he barked out a few brisk orders, dispatching some of his knights to enter and search each building and hut. "The villagers must be persuaded to return with us to the castle where they will be safe," he said. "But go gently. So great will be their terror that even we will be suspect."

Riding down the path in the central part of the village, he saw the smoking remains of several thatched-roof cottages, the dairy, and the blacksmith's hut. But not a solitary soul was in view. They must be huddled inside, poor souls. Or worse still—dead.

Suddenly he was aware of a fluttering movement through the open doorway of a merchant building. "Ho, there! Are you friend or foe?" There was not a sound. Perhaps it was one of the enemy soldiers, caught in the act of looting. On the other hand, it could be a villager.

"If you are one of us, we mean you no harm. We've come to give you safe escort back to the castle."

In a moment, a sallow-faced, middle-aged woman emerged, holding onto the doorframe, her features contorted with pain and horror.

"Good woman, get you to the castle, where you may find sanctuary."

"I cannot leave my husband," she said, despair ravaging her voice.

"He is welcome as well. Is he inside?"

"He is dead. All of the merchants are dead, save me."

"Then praise be to God who has spared you," he said, not knowing what more to say to ease her grief.

"I hid in the cellar. They did not find me, for the door is underneath the bed. I could hear all the screaming. . .and did not come out to help. I stayed there and let my husband and neighbors die—" Her voice trailed off in a keening wail.

"There is nothing you could have done, madam. These barbarians are heartless wretches."

Albert's squire caught up with him and waited for his lord to turn to him before speaking. "I caught one rascal and turned him over to the prison squad."

"And here is one of our people who will be glad to hear it. This good woman needs escort to the castle. Make sure she has her belongings with her." He calculated the damage done her establishment with a practiced eye. "It will be some weeks before she can return—and only when the danger is well past."

"And where will you go next, my lord?" the squire asked.

"To the mill to see what might be left of it." Without the mill to grind their barley, rye, and wheat, the villagers could well go hungry come winter.

Albert moved off, but it was only a matter of minutes

before the squire caught up with him again. "My lord, there are so many dead."

Albert glanced sharply at the man, whose usual ruddy complexion had paled to the color of parchment. "Are those who survived now consenting to go behind the castle walls?"

"They are reluctant to leave their loved ones behind. But I think they would be willing to follow us, my lord."

Albert let out a long sigh. "There will be time to bury the dead. But we must make haste to assure that there will be no further loss of life this day."

They rode in silence until the mill was within sight. Before he had come abreast of the oak tree in the bend of the road, Albert could hear the blood-curdling screams of a woman in distress and urged his horse forward, his squire following.

The cries came from within the mill itself, and Albert and his man dismounted. "Tether the horses, then wait here."

With that, he drew his sword and hurried into the mill. Inside, he found the miller and his daughter pressed back against the wall, their faces white with terror. The girl had blood streaming across her face. Their attacker, his unsheathed sword in his hand, whirled to face Albert.

Albert was grateful for the protection of full armor, though it made him ungainly, for this one was obviously a seasoned fighting man, all scars and wariness.

Albert's rage fueled the fight in him, and he struck the first blow, which was expertly parried by his opponent. In fact, to his dismay, Albert could not land a single thrust at first, so deftly did his enemy counter every move.

"Is the fine knight getting tired now?" the soldier taunted. "Drop your sword and I will give you a little rest."

Intrigued by the man's accent—one he could not identify—Albert attempted to keep up the conversation. To do so might be crucial to discovering the identity of the invaders.

"You have a fine voice, ruffian. Likely you are a singer,"

Albert baited him, hoping he would give himself away before dying.

"I am the delight of every girl back home," the man boasted, momentarily dropping his guard. "These women here in Bavaria are nothing but simpering fools."

Albert pressed his advantage and backed the soldier to the wall, then finished him quickly. Glancing about the room, he called out to the miller, crouched between his daughter and the body of the fallen soldier. "Miller, are there any more of these cursed soldiers in the place?"

"No one, my lord. Only this one. But he has caused harm enough," he croaked out in a raspy voice.

Albert approached gingerly, not wishing to alarm them. The girl slid down against the wall, as though her legs were too weak to hold her. Her face was so pale, the blood streaked it almost black in contrast.

"Is there wine or ale in the house?" he asked.

"I don't know," the miller whispered.

Seeing the small dwelling next to the mill, Albert entered, found a gourd, and filled it with water from a pail. He carried it to the miller. "Good miller, give this to the girl."

The miller obeyed, and she sipped. "My only living child," he explained. "My wife died of a fever last winter, thanks be to God, for what has happened here this day would have sent her to her grave."

"Perhaps I can be of some help. May I speak with your daughter?"

The miller nodded and blinked, his red-rimmed eyes tragic in his white face.

"Misstress—?" Doe-brown eyes-a study in grief-flickered to his for a moment and then away. "She does not seem to want to talk now. But we'd best find the source of this bleeding. Did she strike her head?"

The miller examined his daughter's face and neck, running

stubby, yet gentle fingers over her head. "Seems the bleeding stopped," he said. "That knave struck her. And—".His voice broke. "Worse."

Albert took a steadying breath. "Would that you had both been at the castle."

"Hilda begged me to go," the miller howled in remorse, "but I refused. Business has been brisk, and I had wheat to grind. 'Tis my fault this shame has come upon her."

"Peace, miller. This is the fault of these barbarians, none other," he said, nodding toward the lifeless body on the floor.

The girl glanced over at the soldier and began to retch. Her father cradled her head, and wept.

Albert left the pitiful scene to speak with his squire who was waiting under a tree outside. "What news here?"

"Two of the men have reported few survivors," he said. "The strike was thorough, if brief." He surveyed his leader with a quizzical look. "What happened in there?"

"A ruffian injured a girl. He will not do it again. He spoke with an accent of some kind. I will question the merchant woman. Perhaps she heard it, too, and can tell us what she makes of it."

"Did you not keep him alive for questioning?"

Albert shrugged. "It could not be helped. I had to work quickly, or more lives would have been lost. The girl will need transport to the castle. Stand guard, and do not allow anyone to cross this threshold."

When Albert returned to the miller and his daughter, he found them somewhat calmer. "I will arrange for your daughter to be taken to the castle for safekeeping. Will you go with us?" he asked the miller.

But it was the daughter who answered. "No!" she moaned. "Please don't carry me away from my home!"

Albert eyed her skeptically. "Why not? There is a healer, a gentlewoman who will tend your wound."

The young woman sighed and met his gaze. "People will know what has happened to me and will talk. I would not disgrace my father."

"Nonsense. You have disgraced no one. You are hurt and need attention."

"Could I go somewhere else?" The dark eyes were brilliant with tears.

"Please, sir knight," the miller begged. "My daughter has suffered enough humiliation."

Albert pondered his dilemma. He could not leave his post to take this young woman to some remote region. "I could have a man take you to my parents' home."

She began to weep, and whispered something to her father.

"She trusts no one but you, sir," he said in a plaintive voice.

There was no need for further speculation. "Then I will escort you personally to my parents' keep," Albert said decisively. "We'll be off as soon as my squire has located some blankets."

Outside, there was a hasty conference with the squire. "I will be making a quick trip to Beroburg, it seems. I need you to ride ahead of me to let them know what has happened here today and to alert the physician. I am certain that our message went astray last night, else Father would have sent help." Spotting one of his knights, Albert beckoned to him, and he came straightaway.

"Yes, my lord?"

"I will be away for a few hours. I'm leaving you in command of this operation. Evacuate the rest of the village and bring them to the castle. I'll go for help."

❧

When a minor incident in the chapel called Father Bernard from her lesson, Margarethe went looking for her aunt in the solar. Lady Mechthild was gazing out the window overlooking the bailey where Lord Einhard was addressing his men in the field. "What is Uncle doing?" she asked.

'Lady Mechthild put her arm around Margarethe's slender shoulders. "He is asking them if they would be willing to join Otto's forces in their fight."

"Oh," Margarethe breathed. "Then maybe my dream was true."

Puzzled, Mechthild drew back to regard her niece. "What dream?"

"I could not sleep, so I was praying. As I asked God to direct my prayers, I fell asleep. I dreamed that Albert was riding through a village weeping in despair. The village was in ruins, and there were bodies everywhere."

"What then?"

"I woke to a strong desire to pray for Lord Otto's men, but especially for Albert."

Lady Mechthild looked stricken, and reached inside her long sleeve to withdraw a piece of paper. "Read this. It's from Willem."

Margarethe scanned the letter. "There is great danger, Aunt. Both Willem and I sensed it when we were in prayer. Uncle needs to send help right away."

"Then we must tell him at once."

But when they looked, they found the men dispersing. Without waiting to consult her aunt, Margarethe flung back the shutter and cried, "Uncle Einhard! Wait! Don't send the men away!"

Rushing down the stairs, followed by Lady Mechthild, she ran out to greet him, pulled him aside, and told him of her dream.

Lord Einhard stared hard in concentration, then strode back to his troops, calling them to attention. "The situation has changed. We must prepare to defend Beroburg. We leave at once."

&

Willem was working on some music for the entertainment of some special guests when a page dashed into the hall in search of Lord Otto. "Troops approaching, my lord!"

"From what direction?"

"From the east, sir."

For the first time, Otto smiled. "Einhard." Looking immensely relieved, he rose and quickly left the hall.

"Thank You, Father," Willem breathed, striking a chord to harmonize with the prayer he sent heavenward.

seven

Willem ran to the door to hear the news when it was rumored that Lord Albert's squire had ridden in alone—the first sign that something was very wrong. When Willem learned that the village had been attacked and the message system had failed, he was appalled. Even more so when, in lowered tones, the squire told Lord Otto of a savage crime committed against a village girl.

Lord Otto called Jolan over at once. "I hope you don't mind delaying your visit home for a while. I will need your healing skills for an unfortunate young woman."

"Of course, Uncle," she murmured. "I'll help in any way I can."

He gave her a grim smile, then inclined his head toward the squire. "See that a page carries your message to the physician, then get some dinner. You have ridden hard and long."

"I beg your pardon, my lord, but I need to get back to Lord Albert."

"We will see Albert soon enough. Right now we must summon my knights for a war council."

❧

Lord Einhard's entire household was in a state of chaos at the news that their soldiers would be joining Otto's war. Lady Mechthild, in particular. She had not expected her husband to accompany his troops, and Margarethe could tell that her aunt had been weeping, along with countless other women—from chambermaids to knights' ladies.

So it was that Margarethe made a bold suggestion. "I know it is not the usual time of day for songs in the hall, Aunt, but perhaps it would help to ease the tension."

Mechthild nodded thoughtfully. "A good idea. We could have some music before the dinner hour. Let's sing some of the psalms to fortify our hearts."

Margarethe called over two of the other musicians, who helped gather a few instruments. They started with the psalms as her aunt had suggested, and went on to some other uplifting tunes. Indeed, some said later, it was as if a blanket of peace had descended over that portion of the hall where the stringed instruments and voices blended in celestial music.

≥∘

"Come with me, Willem, and sing us off," Lord Otto said as he strode to his waiting horse.

This was no invitation; rather, it was a direct command. With his horse saddled and ready, Willem mounted, accepting his lute as if it were a saber from the hand of a servant who stood by.

At Lord Otto's signal, he advanced to the head of the troops just outside the gate, listened to a brief rallying speech, then led out in the fiercest battle song he knew, followed by an invocation of God's blessing on their efforts that day.

As the troops paraded by, banners streaming in the balmy breeze and lances poised, Willem watched with a kind of mingled pride and dread. So many men. But how many would return at battle's end?

The last man rode by, and Willem turned to ride back to the castle when Lord Otto halted him with an upraised arm. "Stay. That must be Albert coming. We'll hear what he has to say."

Near the outskirts of the village, a cloud of dust signaled an approaching horseman. As the rider drew nearer, Willem could see that he was carrying something that appeared to be the figure of a woman, slumped forward in the saddle in front of him.

"Father, well-met. Greetings, Willem," Albert hailed them.

At close range, Willem could see that the maiden's face, bearing the pallor of battle shock, was badly bruised and she was trembling. She did not meet their gaze, but glanced quickly away.

"Father, this woman was attacked by one of the enemy soldiers. I have brought her here to recover. She is Hilda, daughter to the miller."

"Greetings, Hilda. Would that we had met under more pleasant circumstances. But you will be avenged—that I can promise you."

"My lord Albert has already avenged me," she said softly, "and it is enough."

Lord Otto then turned his attention to his son. "Did you discover why the relay system failed?"

"The second messenger was murdered moments after receiving the message. I found his body and that of his horse not a furlong from the relay point."

"Then we should have had a backup messenger. Einhard and his troops have just ridden out with ours."

Willem noticed that Hilda shifted a little in her seat.

Albert glanced at her and nudged the horse forward. "That is good news. How did he know to come?"

Lord Otto and Willem fell in beside him, and they rode three abreast. "Willem wrote of our troops' sad lack of morale."

"So, you are visiting then, Willem?"

"Ah. . .no. Your father has prevailed—"

"Willem has consented to join our household," Lord Otto said with surprising pride. "He wrote Einhard to ask for troops for the next battle. When young Margarethe revealed a dream she had last night Einhard and his troops rode out at once."

As Lord Otto was speaking, Willem watched Hilda's eyes grow large and fearful.

"A dream? How so?"

"Apparently she fell asleep while she was praying." Otto recounted the details as he recalled them.

Albert nodded in understanding. "Margarethe has always seen more than others. Would that she could join our household as well."

"God grant that it may be so," his father agreed.

Willem felt a flush heat his cheeks, then caught Hilda stealing a glance at him.

"Father, one of the foot soldiers spoke with a strange accent. There is a merchant woman among my people at the castle. Perhaps she heard it and can help us."

"And the foot soldier?"

There was a long pause. "In self-defense, I was forced to kill him." He cast Hilda a quick look, and she squeezed her eyes shut. "There must be others in the prison who could be interrogated. Meanwhile, we have work to do right here."

Lord Otto nodded. "It is a good thing Jolan had not left for her journey home to visit her parents and Margarethe. Her healing skills will be of help to our miller's daughter."

Albert looked thoughtful. "Yes, and Margarethe would also be a good companion for Hilda. They are about the same age and Margarethe's gifts would be helpful to her."

"Let us send for her then."

Once more Willem had to restrain his emotions, lest his face betray his heart. They rode in silence to the very door of the donjon, where Lord Otto waved off a bevy of curious servants.

In his heavy armor, Willem suspected that Lord Albert would have difficulty in dismounting, with the maiden still clasped in his arms. But when Lord Otto instructed his son to hand Hilda down to him, she leaned hard against the young lord and clung to his surcoat.

Lord Otto appeared completely bewildered.

"The maiden has learned to trust me alone, Father," Albert

explained. "But we do have a problem, Maid Hilda," he said, leaning down to speak gently. "You will have to allow someone else to carry you until I can rid myself of this breastplate."

"Forgive me, my lord," she whispered back. "Can Lord Willem help?"

At the nod, Willem hastened to dismount, handed his lute to a servant, and put up his arms to lift Hilda down from the horse's back.

"Use care, Willem," Albert cautioned. "She is injured and cannot stand."

Willem gathered her into his arms and waited while Albert dismounted. But before he knew what was happening, a flash of blue whirled past. It was Jolan, Margarethe's young friend. She took both Albert's hands and stood on tiptoe to kiss his cheek.

"Albert," she cried, "I am so sorry about your village and your people."

Albert appeared not at all flustered, but immediately took her into his confidence. "Greetings, Jolan. This is Hilda, the miller's daughter. She will need rest and quiet and the ministrations of a physician. But in the meantime, I thought you might befriend her," he said under his breath.

Hilda regarded the trembling girl with great sympathy. "Bring her to my chamber. It is more private than the infirmary." She looked at Hilda, lying in Willem's arms. "You will be quite safe with us, and well in no time."

And with that, Jolan led the way to her chamber, where she ensconced the maid in her own bed and covered her tenderly.

❧

As the servitors brought in trays laden with steaming venison soup for the noon meal, Margarethe arranged for an hour of rehearsal in the banquet hall after dinner. Even Lady Mechthild agreed to be one of the players. If nothing else, Margarethe thought, the diversion would provide her aunt a welcome respite from thoughts of the war.

She sat beside Lady Mechthild at table and talked a little with young Friedrich who was permitted to join them today.

"Cousin, do you remember how to catch frogs?" he asked, leaning up on his elbows to speak to her around his mother.

Margarethe laughed at the child, his impish face all ears and earnestness. "I suspect I'm a little out of practice."

"Well, you should have caught up on your music at least after this afternoon's rehearsal," her aunt observed.

Margarethe dipped her head in a little bow. "I count it my small contribution to the cause, Aunt."

"Cousin, I would be honored to help you practice catching frogs," the boy persisted.

She stifled a smile. "How thoughtful of you, Friedrich. But we should wait until the weather is warmer, and we can hear them singing in the rushes. Then we'll know for sure where to look for them."

Friedrich pursed his lips in a pout. "They never sing until almost May Day. And that's such a long time from now."

You're wrong, young Friedrich, Margarethe thought to herself. *May Day will come all too soon.*

❧

Troubled by the events of the past day, Jolan rose early the next morning for Mass. It was not her usual custom, but extraordinary circumstances required extraordinary measures. In assisting the physician, she had learned the nature of all of Hilda's injuries. Of course, she was no child and had heard of such things. But to sit and talk with someone who had suffered such an atrocity was new to her.

If Hilda recovered quickly, she knew that Albert would be greatly encouraged. And so she prayed—out of pity for the maid, out of love for her favorite male cousin. Still, it was Margarethe who was her true favorite.

How she wished they could be together now. Margarethe

and her parents had invited her for a visit, and she would have left this very day, except for this dreadful turn of events. Now Hilda needed her, and there was no help for it but to stay. She could not be so selfish as to leave on a holiday, or even to beg Margarethe to come here instead. She must do her duty. Albert had requested it himself.

"Help me, Father God," she whispered into the near-empty chapel. "I have no wisdom in such things. Tell me what to do. Or send someone else to help Hilda. She cries all the time, and I don't know how to comfort her."

Jolan noticed that Willem, too, was attending Mass and wondered if he came often, or only when he was in trouble as she did. No, that couldn't be. Willem was older and wiser and could handle anything.

Leaving the chapel, Jolan allowed Willem to catch up with her, using his familiar springy step. "Good morning, my lady. How is your patient?"

"She is quiet this morning, thanks be to God. But she cried most of the night. I'm at my wits' end as to how to help her."

"And so you have come to the chapel to pray. A very good start indeed. I trust God will answer all your prayers, my lady."

"Thank you, Willem," she answered, her cheeks warm. "I hope God answers all your prayers as well."

He walked at her side in silent speculation, then spoke up. "If I recall correctly, you are to have a voice lesson today. When would you be available?"

Jolan shook her head. "I don't know when Hilda might sleep, and I don't want to leave her. Since the. . .incident. . . she seems afraid of men—" Suddenly, realizing what she had said, she clapped her hand over her mouth.

"No matter, Jolan. I know what happened to her. She trusts me, it seems. Perhaps we could have your lesson in your chamber, where Hilda could listen."

The idea was pleasing, and Jolan hurried back to tell Hilda of the plan.

The maiden's eyes grew round. "I would be most happy to hear you sing, my lady, if your voice is as fine as your cousin's."

"Oh, it's not nearly as fine as Margarethe's. She has true talent."

"Margarethe? I know no Margarethe. I was speaking of Lord Albert."

"Oh." Jolan laughed. "I suppose his voice is fair. When did you hear him sing?"

"Yesterday, on the ride from the village. He sang lullabies and other soothing melodies."

Jolan nodded and smoothed her skirts. "I remember hearing him sing to me when I was small. He treated like a little princess in those days. He always had time for me."

"And that is why you love him," Hilda stated matter-of-factly.

Jolan felt her eyes widen. "I love him because. . .well, because he is Albert. He's a good and gallant man."

"Will you marry him then?" Hilda asked quietly.

"Oh, no. Our family does not believe in cousins marrying. But he will make a fine husband—Margarethe's, I hope."

"I thought she was a cousin, too." Hilda was clearly puzzled.

Jolan smiled. "It's quite complicated, but I'll try to explain. My father, Lord Einhard, is Margarethe's mother's brother. But Albert's father, Lord Otto, is my mother's brother. So, you see, Margarethe and I are cousins, but she and Albert are not."

Hilda blinked and put her hand to her head. "That will take some pondering."

"While you are pondering, I had best go to table before they decide I am not coming at all." Jolan rose and patted Hilda's hand. "And when I return, I'll bring Willem with me, and we will make music. A merry heart is just the medicine you need."

❧

Margarethe was summoned to Lady Mechthild's chamber shortly before dinner. "Sit down, Greta," her aunt invited, holding a letter in her hands. "This is from Lady Edeltraud, suggesting you come at once. There is something of an emergency at Beroburg."

"Oh. I thought Jolan was coming here to visit," Margarethe said, holding her breath. What if something had happened to Willem?

"The plans have changed. Albert brought in a young maiden who had been violated by one of the enemy soldiers. She is in need of healing in body and in spirit. Jolan is caring for her, but Albert and Otto both felt you might be of some help."

Margarethe frowned. "I don't like leaving you alone, Aunt, with only Friedrich and your maids," she said, but it was Willem she was thinking of. How could she bear to be near him again, knowing they could never wed?

"Don't be concerned about me, my dear." She waved one smooth hand. "I will be fine. I know you have been missing Jolan's company. I wonder, though, if it would be painful—seeing Willem again."

How like Aunt Mechthild. Reading her like a book. Margarethe sighed. "It would be difficult. But we have agreed never to be alone, so that will help."

"Jolan knows nothing of your feelings for Willem, I hope." Margarethe shook her head.

"Then I trust you can keep your feelings to yourself." Lady Mechthild gave a wry smile. "Even if she is my daughter, I will have to say that Jolan is not known for her discretion, and Edeltraud has enough on her mind without dealing with matters of the heart."

"Have no fear, Aunt. Jolan is also easy to distract."

"You're right, my dear." Lady Mechthild gave a little laugh, rose, and tapped the parchment against the palm of her hand. "Then I will write Edeltraud while you gather your things. Sir Johan will escort you. His ankle will not permit him to engage in battle, but he can ride with you. Is that suitable?"

Margarethe rolled her eyes. "As long as he will promise not to taunt me with tales of his recent victories in chess!"

❧

Jolan's singing lesson went well, but Willem found himself frequently glancing in Hilda's direction, fearful that she might be tiring of hearing the scales sung in a less than perfect pitch. Her eyes were closed much of the time, and he could not tell if she were asleep or listening.

"One last song together, Lady Jolan," Willem said, "and then it will be dinnertime."

Hearing a gasp, Willem turned toward the bed, where Maid Hilda was sitting upright.

"What is it, Hilda?" Jolan asked, rushing over to comfort her.

"Forgive me. But it can't be time for dinner. You've only just begun to sing!"

Jolan laughed and Willem chuckled gently. "I think that our guest likes music very much," he said.

"Oh, it would be my life," she said, clasping her hands together. "But I have no training."

"Then, when you're feeling better, you shall have some," Willem promised.

At that moment they heard a noise in the bailey, and Jolan went to the window to look out. "It's the messenger back from Mutti. I hope it is the news I've been waiting for," she said.

They sang one last song, a cheerful song of spring that

Willem had chosen especially for Hilda's benefit. During the last verse and chorus, he noticed a page standing by the door.

The lad waited for the song to end, then sprang forward. "Lady Jolan, Lady Edeltraud would have you know that your cousin is coming this afternoon, as she requested."

Jolan jumped to her feet, laughing in delight. "Margarethe! The answer to my prayers!"

Willem stood, scarcely able to breathe. *And to mine*, he thought.

eight

Willem spoke little during dinner, to the disgust of his dining partner, who had chosen her place opposite him hoping to be the recipient of his renowned wit.

But the only person on his mind was Margarethe. He had not expected to see her so soon after leaving Adlerschloss. He had thought there would be time to adjust to her absence. She was coming, of course, to help with Hilda, whose care was a little daunting for Jolan. Still, he wondered what the great God—He who arranges all things—must be thinking to allow them to meet again so soon.

Sweet Margarethe. He knew her every feature, her every thought and feeling. She had hidden nothing from him in nearly two years, when they had first spoken openly of their love.

Once Margarethe's sense of humor had matured beyond childish pranks, she had developed a delightful ability to mimic various castle visitors with an artful expression or hand gesture discreetly rendered behind her veil. It was often all Willem could do to keep a straight face when she imitated some speaker who droned on past all endurance.

Sometimes her mischief was turned on him. At such times, her teasing kept him both amused and embarrassed by turns. One hot day they had gone for a ride on horseback through the countryside, stopping by a creek to rest. Hoping to cool themselves, they had waded into the water. "I don't suppose you would consent to going for a swim with me?" she had asked, her eyes demurely downcast.

But when he had bent over to see if she might be truly serious, she had splashed him, giggling like the young girl he had known for so long.

He chuckled in remembrance, drawing the curiosity of the woman seated across from him. "Were you daydreaming, sir?" she asked with a coy expression.

"Do forgive me. I was merely thinking of going for a swim."

She dropped her mouth, baffled by his answer, and immediately left off any further questions for the remainder of the meal.

❧

Margarethe wondered what it would be like to see Willem again. He had been in her heart constantly since their parting, and she looked forward to the moment. But it would be quite different, she knew. For one thing, he was no longer her music teacher. For another, she must treat him as she did any other gentleman, neither seeking him out nor paying him any special attention should they chance to meet. While they would be able to carry on a conversation from time to time, she must take care not to be alone with him, lest her emotions run away with her. What agony—this forbidden love!

It was amazing that now they would again be face to face—though not heart to heart or lip to lip. Never that. Never again.

She wrenched her thoughts from what could never be to the task at hand. She would need to pack only a few clothes for herself. But on the chance that the miller's daughter would need something to wear, having left her home so hurriedly, Margarethe added a few garments that had grown too short for her. Since there were instruments aplenty at Lord Otto's, she would take only her lute.

Jolan would be able to use some help in the use of herbs, so Margarethe also packed her precious copy of *Causae et Curae,* by Abbess Hildegard of Bingen. The book contained all sorts of useful information, and had been given to her by Father Bernard who had painstakingly transcribed the copy himself from a copy his sister had obtained at the very abbey in which Abbess Hildegard lived and worked a hundred and fifty years before.

Finally, Margarethe put in a few dried herbs from the castle infirmary. What with treating battle wounds and injuries, no doubt such supplies would be scarce at Beroburg.

On the road with Sir Johan and his squire, Margarethe saw that the daffodils were blooming at the edges of the woods. The sweet smell wafted to them on the breeze, the cheerful yellow heads bobbing in time to the music of the skylark. Though the birds of early spring were fewer in number than they would be in the merry month of May, their song seemed all the sweeter.

So lovely was the day and so fragrant the flowers that before they reached Lord Otto's castle, Margarethe asked her escorts to stop so that she might pick daffodils for Jolan and Lady Edeltraud. Pleading his sore ankle, Sir Johan remained on his horse. But his squire willingly dismounted to help gather armfuls of the flowers.

Upon their arrival at the castle, Jolan was waiting to greet her, quickly followed by Lady Edeltraud and a swarm of maids and pages, who bustled about to carry in the trunks and bundles.

"So the late snow did not kill them, after all," observed Lady Edeltraud, burying her nose in the buttery yellow blossoms. "Come in, child. Have you dined? And you, sir," she said to Johan and his squire, "you are both welcome at our table."

"Thank you, my lady, but we have eaten," he said pointedly, directing his words to the young man whose countenance fell.

Margarethe smiled up at him. "I thank you for bringing me here, Sir Johan. I hope your ankle heals quickly and that you will soon be able to go on to more interesting duties."

Still mounted on his horse, he bowed. "I shall miss our

chess games. You are a worthy opponent, my lady."

"Oh, I intend to improve still more. I shall be practicing here with some truly great players. So the next time we meet, you'd best be on your guard."

He bowed again, reined his horse around, and rode away, his laughter trailing over his shoulder.

In all the commotion, Margarethe had not yet laid eyes on Willem. She spotted him as she and Jolan, her arms laden with flowers for Hilda, were starting through the back of the great hall on the way to her chamber. He came straight over, offering to carry Margarethe's lute.

"So, you've come to visit then?" he asked, his eyes all merriment and love.

She shrugged, trying for an indifferent attitude, and failing miserably. "Jolan needed me to help with that poor village girl, and so I came."

"That's good. Jolan and I have found that the patient loves music, and she is quite wearing us out with her requests. Now you may take a turn."

"Willem, don't be ridiculous," Jolan chided. "She is hardly wearing us out. Margarethe, don't listen to him." Casting about, she gave a great sigh. "I need a large container for these flowers. Now where are all those lazy pages anyway?"

"Ah, I think they are carrying Lady Margarethe's things to her chamber, my lady," Willem reminded her.

Margarethe knew his thoughts, knew that he was repressing a big grin.

"Well, I will just have to find one myself," Jolan said, dumped the daffodils into Margarethe's arms, and flounced off.

"I know the way, my lady. I will take you there," Willem said, his hand light on her back. He glanced around the hall, then lowered his voice. "It may not be wise to count on Jolan for escort. She is a flighty one."

Margarethe laughed lightly. "She has ever been so. But I cannot see around these flowers. Do not let me trip on anything on my way up the stairs."

"Then let me take them." He slung the lute on its strap around to his back and held out his arms for the flowers, his hand grazing hers in the transfer.

"Oh, Willem," she breathed. "Will there be any time for us? Any time to make music as we once did?"

His gaze was tender. "I'm sure of it." Margarethe noticed that his tone was still measured and respectfully distant—as they had agreed—though it grieved her to hear it. "The people in this household love music. I will be playing every Lord's Day and many other times as well. Perhaps there will even be an occasional day off when I can pursue my own pleasure."

Margarethe smiled over at him. "And what would you do with a day off, sir?"

"I would write music and make new arrangements and catch up. . ."

"Watch out!" Margarethe warned. "We are coming to the first step now." She laughed as Willem groped blindly with his foot. "Do you perform all your silliness for Lord Otto's house as you did at home?"

"Of course. I even sang a duet with Gregor—your future husband—while he was in the bathtub."

Margarethe did not dare respond to such a remark, and rushed a few steps ahead, then turned to confront him. "Willem," she said softly but sternly, "there are things you should not tease me about."

He gazed at her sadly. "You are right. Please forgive me, my lady."

"Of course, I forgive you," she said, striving for a lighter tone. "And if you are agreeable, I will even join your musical group and help you out."

"Now that would be a boon indeed—a welcome change

from some around here who aspire to make music, but do not possess your gifting."

Reaching the top of the stairs. Willem led Margarethe to a chamber door and paused outside. "Maid Hilda? It is Willem and Margarethe. May we come in?"

"Enter," came a small voice, whispery-soft.

They entered the room, Willem partially obscured behind the mass of flowers in his arms, while Margarethe advanced toward the bed. She felt a rush of pity for the young woman lying there with that great bruise on her face, doubtless more hidden beneath the bed coverings, and untold bruises in her spirit.

"I am Margarethe," she introduced herself. "If I know Jolan, you have heard all about me."

"Greetings, my lady. I hope you had a pleasant journey."

"It was a fine day for a ride. And just look what we found along the way. Jolan has gone for a container."

"Lady Jolan has told me that you are very talented. . .in music. She and Willem have been so kind to let me listen to them practice."

Willem cleared his throat. "The three of us together are even better. And just wait until you hear Margarethe sing with Jolan. Even the angels stoop to listen."

Margarethe was laughing when Jolan burst into the room with a crockery jar for the flowers, took them from Willem and plopped them unceremoniously into the water, sloshing a bit of it onto the floor.

Jolan stood back a little to admire the effect while Willem found a towel and mopped up the spill. "There, Hilda. Margarethe has brought the outdoors in." Turning to Willem, she said, "Would you please step out for a minute? We ladies must talk."

He gave a little bow. "I'll be right outside if you should need me."

"Yes, yes. I'll call you. Now go." She gave him a little push and turned to Hilda as soon as he had closed the door. "Now, Hilda, you have been in bed for some time. Do you need anything—perhaps to use the privy or take a bath?"

"Oh, please. I would be so grateful. But the bath can wait as long as we can have music."

Margarethe and Jolan helped her out of bed to tend to the necessities. "You shall have music," Jolan promised. "Then before supper, we will see about some other things to make you more comfortable."

When Hilda was settled back in bed, they called Willem in. This time, he brought in his lute and a leather bag of wind instruments. "I thought Maid Hilda might enjoy a small concert."

No comment was necessary. Her joy was reflected in her radiant face as she clasped her hands together in anticipation.

"Is there anything special you would like to hear?" Margarethe asked.

"Does anyone play the viel? It makes such a lovely sound."

"I will fetch a couple of viels from the music chamber," Willem said. "Jolan can observe this time," he added with a rueful grin.

"I have inherited my mother's lack of congeniality with the viel, I'm afraid. She is like Margarethe—she can play any instrument. Any instrument but the viel, that is."

"Jolan, we have not sung together in months," Margarethe reminded her. "We should warm up while we wait for Willem. You start."

Jolan began one of their old favorites—a round with three verses. On the second, Margarethe spotted Willem waiting at the door. When Jolan began a new phrase, he took up the melody, then joined in the third verse to finish the exercise.

There was laughter at the song's conclusion except for Maid Hilda, who breathed, "Wunderbar!"

Willem handed Margarethe a viel, and they tuned up. "What shall we play?"

"I was playing *"Dominus Vobiscum"* with Aunt Mechthild and Father Bernard yesterday when a new song came to me in the same mode. Could we play the old song? Then I will play the new one, and you can join me the second time through."

The first melody—slow and stately—soared to its majestic conclusion, the two viels in close harmony. Afterward, Willem dropped out and allowed Margarethe to play the new tune. As planned, he joined her, blending in a simple harmony. The song ended on a sustained note that rose past the vaulted ceiling and into the heavens, it seemed.

"Oh, Margarethe," Jolan said, "I've never heard anything so lovely."

Willem, too, was moved. "Have you written a lyric?"

"Not yet," she replied and noticed that tears were rolling down Hilda's cheeks. She hurried to comfort her. "Oh, I'm so sorry that the music made you sad."

"Oh, my lady, it's just that it was so beautiful—and now I am wondering how people like you, who can create such beauty, could care for me?"

"It is no mystery. You are one of God's precious ones, and we love you. It's as simple as that."

Jolan bustled over with a handkerchief. "Uncle Otto told me of a new love song you and Willem have been singing, Margarethe. I want to hear it. Would you like that, Hilda?"

"Yes, please," she said. Jolan sat beside her on the bed, one hand resting lightly on Hilda's arm, the other making a commanding gesture in the air. "Then let the music begin."

Margarethe picked up her lute and found it already tuned. *How like Willem to be so thoughtful,* she thought, feeling another pang in her heart.

He picked up his own lute and laid a soprano recorder where he could reach it and nodded to her. They sang that song, played the instrumental passage without a flaw, and seeing Hilda's obvious delight, sang the chorus an extra time, ending with a repeat of the last four lines.

> 'Til all our days shall pass,
>   We'll be together, you and me.
> As ever on the brook flows down
>   Constant to the sea.
> As it's renewed by snow and rain,
>   Our love's fed from above.

"I always will be true to you," Willem sang in his rich tenor, and Margarethe answered in her sweet alto: "You'll always be my love."

Only when the sun sank low in the western sky did they stop to care for Hilda's needs. But even with the other women in the room, Margarethe's heart was bonded with Willem's once more—as if they had never been apart.

nine

With the troops coming home the next day—the Lord's Day—Jolan had to plead for enough hot water for Hilda to bathe. While servants brought in great kettles of water, heated over the fire, Margarethe made an infusion of soothing herbs to sprinkle in the bath. Hilda would be able to soak her aching muscles instead of sponging off as was the custom. But to everyone's surprise, the men arrived early, making a great commotion in the vaulted halls.

Jolan was relieved to hear the shouting and joshing among the men. "When the battle goes poorly, they come home sullen and silent. This noise is a good sign," she explained.

"I hope all continues to go well for them, though I must admit I do not understand this war at all."

Jolan was quick to supply a brief overview of the turbulent history of their border. "Back when all this started, Uncle Otto and a few others noticed that we had too many robberies on the roads. Uncle sent out some of his men disguised as merchants to see what was going on. From their report, he suspected that these were not ordinary thieves. Indeed, it turns out they were Lord Ewald's men all along."

"But I heard that Lord Ewald and his allies were stopping people on the road and demanding huge tolls."

"True—" Jolan looked off as if deciding whether to continue— "along with other crimes. And in exchange for the tolls, the travelers were offered protection from the robbers."

"What gall!"

"Exactly. Of course, Uncle Otto and the other honest people asked Lord Ewald to stop this abominable practice.

When he refused, Uncle and his allies broke off trade relations. Unfortunately, this only fueled Ewald's resolve to steal even more."

"Why is it that so many goods pass through this area?" Hilda put in for the first time.

Ah, a hopeful sign, Margarethe thought. That the maiden should take an interest in something besides her own sad plight was a small indicator of her recovery.

"The east-west road that intersects the valley is a major trade route," Jolan explained. "It connects with several other well-traveled roads. Or they would be—if not for the threat of robbers—and this awful war."

She rose to straighten Hilda's bed coverings. "And the north-south route that links Bavaria with the other German lands runs straight through the disputed valley."

Margarethe was now curious about this war she had long disdained to be informed about. "Jolan, what other crimes did Lord Ewald commit besides the robberies and collecting tolls he wasn't entitled to?"

"He is cruel to Jews. He taxes them more heavily than others. And one night in Rogensruhe, when he burned their homes and shops, many lost their lives."

Margarethe was horrified. "How could he do such a thing?"

Jolan shrugged. "I can't fathom it myself. But I do know it triggered the war, for Ewald himself had a large house in Rogensruhe, filled with lovely things, and—"

Margarethe snorted. "Most of them stolen, no doubt."

"Someone went to Ewald's house in Rogensruhe and burned it, just as he had done to the Jews," Jolan continued. "Assuming the deed was ordered by Uncle Otto, Ewald retaliated by declaring war."

"And was it true—that your uncle ordered the burning, I mean?" Hilda asked in a soft voice.

"I don't know, but someone I trust says Uncle was not

displeased when it happened."

Then Jolan told Margarethe of the recent attack on Albert's village. "Hilda could tell us more—if she's willing," she said, glancing toward the pale girl propped against the pillows. "Sometimes it helps to share the things that trouble us most."

Hesitantly at first, but with growing confidence, Hilda related the whole sordid story, reducing them all to tears before she was through.

"I'm glad you felt you could share your pain with us," Margarethe said. "And we are both here if you care to say more."

"Thank you, my lady," Hilda murmured. "You and Lord Albert are so kind to take a stranger into your family." She eyed Margarethe with a puzzled expression. "But then you are not a true cousin to him, if I understand correctly."

Jolan grinned and bobbed up from the stool where she was sitting to poke at the fire. "We are all hoping she will be related soon."

"I will, in truth," Margarethe said with a little sigh. "I am to marry one of Lord Otto's sons."

Hilda's eyes grew wide. "Which one?"

"All four have proposed, but my uncle and father have assured me that I may have my choice when the time comes." Thinking to change the subject, which was always burdensome, Margarethe hurried on. "But shouldn't you get out and dry off? The water is nearly cold by now."

Jolan and Margarethe gently eased Hilda from the tub, wrapped her ribs, helped her into a fresh smock, and tucked her into bed again. All this time Hilda was studying Margarethe with a measured look.

Noticing, Margarethe asked, "Do you have an opinion as to which of Lord Otto's sons I should choose?"

"Oh, no, my lady. I have met only Lord Albert, though I must say he is the finest man I have ever known, save for my father. He rescued me and prayed for me and sang songs to help me forget my ordeal. And all of this without ever mentioning that he was a wealthy and powerful lord. In fact, it was not until we were within sight of Beroburg that it came up at all."

Jolan sat on the bed by Hilda and gestured for Margarethe to do the same. To Margarethe's discomfort, the maiden was still gazing steadily at her. "Albert is a fine man, but I will not tell you which I favor." Margarethe glanced sharply at Jolan. "And you must promise not to tell, either. I would prefer Hilda's unbiased opinion."

"Once you are able to come down to the hall for meals you will be able to meet all of them," Jolan told her. "In the meantime, perhaps we should ask Margarethe what she is looking for in a husband."

The two women waited expectantly while Margarethe gathered her thoughts. "Well, he must be kind—"

"They are all kind!"

"I would like someone who has a good sense of humor," Margarethe went on, overlooking Jolan's interruption.

"Then that lets Klaus out." Jolan again. "He's as sober as a monk."

"Not to mention pompous and self-important," Margarethe added. She grew serious again. "I need someone who honors God, someone who can sing with me and make music whenever the mood strikes."

"Albert," Hilda began, then blushed at the slip of her tongue. "That is, *I* know that *Lord* Albert is a praying man and he likes to sing. He has a most pleasant voice."

"Yes, he does," Jolan agreed. "But Gregor also likes to sing. Now Gottfried, on the other hand, has no sense of pitch, and Klaus can sing, but finds it pointless." Jolan pulled a face that set the others to giggling. "Klaus will need a wife with an excellent sense of humor, for he has none whatsoever."

"It sounds like a choice between Lord Gregor and Lord Albert then," Hilda wisely decided. "And since I have not met Lord Gregor, I suppose I can be of no further help."

Margarethe hesitated, wondering if she should mention her final criterion. "There is one thing more. My husband must be even-tempered. I do not care to be shouted at or abused. Nor could I bear to have my servants or my children mistreated." At this, she watched Hilda's face for evidence that she might have erred in suggesting this ugly reminder of the poor girl's recent experience.

Not surprisingly, a worried look crossed the maiden's face. "That may eliminate Lord Albert, my lady. He was quite angry—justifiably so, of course—but he did kill a man in defending my honor."

There was silence while they pondered the matter. Then Jolan ventured an opinion. "I do think it's the only thing he could have done. Else the brute would have been free to terrorize other maidens. And I have never seen Albert angry—only kind and gentle."

Touched by their concern for her decision, Margarethe wanted to know more. "Jolan, how do you find Gregor's disposition?"

"Oh, I have seen him irritated by small annoyances, but mostly he treats all of life as a great joke. Still, if it were up to me, I would rather have Albert any day."

Margarethe grinned over at her cousin. "I already knew what your opinion would be. You've always adored Albert, followed him around like a puppy." She turned to include Hilda in the conversation. "My cousin was always trying to impress him—plying him with flowers or frogs—"

"Frogs! You should talk about frogs! Hilda, Margarethe was the best frog-catcher around. She would hide them behind her back, then plop them in someone's lap without warning!"

From the smile on Hilda's face, it was clear that she was enjoying the account. Then a sudden frown creased her brow. "Lady Jolan, how old were you when you were following Lord Albert about?"

"Oh, I must have been three or so, and Albert was nine. He's six years older than I."

"Then if you are fourteen, that would make him twenty now—"

Before Jolan could respond, there was a knock at the door and she rushed to answer it. It was a page summoning them for supper.

Margarethe noticed the look of alarm on Hilda's face. "Is something wrong?"

"Nothing, really," she said, picking at the bedclothes. "I'm being silly, I suppose. I'm sure I will be just fine here alone."

"If you feel lonely, we could stay with you during the meal. But after supper, Jolan and I will both be working."

"Working?" Hilda seemed genuinely confused.

"Yes. The men will want music until late at night. I'm afraid we will both be needed in the hall to help Willem," Margarethe said, carefully watching for Hilda's reaction. No doubt the poor thing was frightened of the boisterous soldiers she heard romping about the castle. She certainly had reason to be fearful, after the shameful act that had been forced upon her.

Jolan was quick to sense Hilda's alarm as well. "I'll call a guard. Shall I tell him that only Lord Albert or Willem are to be admitted?"

"Oh, would you, Lady Jolan? I would be ever so grateful." She looked so wan and defenseless lying there. "I do hope you don't think me foolish."

"Of course not. But we shall hope that by tomorrow evening, you will be joining us in the banquet hall. After all, without your counsel, Margarethe cannot make up her mind who is to be the lucky man to claim her hand in marriage."

Willem was relieved to see Lady Jolan and Margarethe taking their places at table. Not yet knowing the full potential of the other castle musicians, he intended to work the two young ladies mercilessly. They would love it!

Right now, observing the warm greetings bestowed on Margarethe by her suitors and the way she responded to each of them with equal warmth, he felt a pang of regret. Why couldn't he be one of those favored few contending for her hand? Still, no one else made music the way the two of them did, and soon she would be singing with him again—even if there was a large audience to hear them.

After supper, Willem called on Margarethe for the first song. They had played for perhaps half an hour when Willem noticed a page running down the stairs and back up again. Following that, another page brought a chair and placed it near the back of the hall.

A lady, supported by the first page, slowly descended the stairs. Even from this distance, he could see that it was Maid Hilda. And when she was seated, he whispered to Margarethe and Jolan, and they struck up a lively tune that the maiden had enjoyed.

While the other musicians were playing and Willem was taking a break, Gregor called him over. "How about that drinking song? We could try a duet if you're agreeable? And Father doesn't mind a little dancing, either, now that the Lenten season is behind us. Perhaps a little Saracen dance music, with the chimes and drums and those wailing shawms. I see some toes already tapping."

Willem bowed. "As you wish. But I'll need Lady Margarethe on the shawms," he teased.

Gregor looked so comically mournful that Willem relented. "Perhaps she won't be needed on all the numbers," he said, at which Lord Gregor's countenance brightened at once.

Willem couldn't help liking Gregor in spite of the fact that this would probably be the man who would take Margarethe from him forever. And he had to wonder what his attitude would have been if he'd known that only a few days ago, Willem had been kissing his intended!

At the end of the song, Willem announced Lord Gregor's request. Tables and benches were pushed against the walls, and the hall cleared for dancing. As the music played, the lord and ladies formed a circle—Saracen-style—and began the ring dance.

Before the first dance had ended, Willem leaned over and spoke into Margarethe's ear. "The next tune will be a couples dance, so I won't need you to play."

"If I don't play, I'll have to dance!" she whispered back fiercely.

"I believe that's the idea."

"How much did Gregor pay you?" she demanded, sounding snappish and not at all like the Greta he knew.

Willem laughed. Better that than speaking his heart. The idea of another man holding her in his arms was too much to bear. So. . .best to get the whole thing over.

He signaled for order as the dance ended, and Margarethe put down her shawm. Instantly, Gregor was at her side, looking smug, and Willem overheard their conversation as he asked Margarethe to dance.

"I'm a very poor dancer, I'm afraid, Gregor," she began. "The music I make requires fingers and lips—not feet. Therefore, I've never learned what to do with them."

"I'll take my chances, my lady," he said with a grin. "Besides, it would give me great pleasure to be your instructor." He gave Willem a sidelong look. "It occurs to me that your tutors have much readier access to you than anyone else."

She appeared to ignore the implication and rushed on. "And for every dance I dance with you, I will have to dance one with each of your brothers as well."

"Then you shall be busy indeed, for I plan to dance with you at least seven times this night. Come, lovely lady."

She allowed him to lead her out onto the floor and even managed a smile as the music began. True to her prediction, she danced the night away—first with each of the brothers in turn, then with Lord Otto and Uncle Einhard, returning to Gregor again and again. It was too much to be endured, Willem thought.

At last, leaving the music to a trio of players who had proved themselves adequate musicians, Willem found the nerve to approach Margarethe. Willingly, she drifted into his light embrace with a whisper of long skirts. He easily spanned her small waist with his hands while she placed her hands on his shoulders. Even in this stiff and formal manner, he was near enough to see the pulse beating in her throat, to smell the sweet gardenia fragrance of her skin. The torchlight cast interesting shadows across the planes of her face as they danced, and she kept her gaze fastened on his until the song ended—much too soon.

Regretting the moment, he bowed low and kissed her hand, then whispered, "Rest for a while, then we'll sing our song for Maid Hilda."

But when he glanced toward the back of the hall, he could see that Hilda's chair was vacant.

⁂

Later, Margarethe and Jolan stole into the chamber where Hilda was staying to see how she was faring. They were surprised to find Albert, sitting beside her and singing softly, accompanying himself on a lute.

"Albert, I didn't know you were here. The poor thing will never recover if you keep her up all night," Jolan scolded.

"She asked for music when I carried her back upstairs from the hall. But she is sleeping now, I think."

"Is there any news from the village?" Margarethe whispered.

"Yes. Good news. More of the people were safe than we thought, for they hid in the woods when they heard the troops coming. We had feared many more casualties—or perhaps even capture."

"Hilda will be so glad to hear that when she wakes up," Margarethe said.

Jolan gave an exaggerated yawn, and taking the cue, Albert rose and placed the lute gently on the table.

"I will let you ladies get your rest now. Let me know if there is something else I can do to be of service."

"We will, Albert," Jolan assured him. "Good night."

"Yes, good night, Albert," Margarethe echoed. "And thank you."

Albert tipped his head. "For what?"

"For caring for Hilda so tenderly, and for absenting yourself from the dancing. It saved me several dances, for which my feet are grateful." She winced.

Albert grinned. "Hilda says that you will choose a husband soon. If you make your choice known, that would save you many dances."

"No doubt it would."

"Klaus was just saying tonight how he'd love to have you as his bride," Albert teased.

Margarethe narrowed her eyes. "Good night, Albert."

He smiled, leaned over and kissed her cheek, then Jolan's, and with a wave of his hand, he was gone.

"Klaus, indeed," Margarethe muttered.

ten

After Mass, Willem greeted Margarethe and motioned for her to sit across from him at table while waiting to break their fast. "How is Maid Hilda this morning?" he asked.

"Sound asleep. I stopped by her chamber to check on her, and Jolan says she cried out but once in the night. She seems to be improving each day."

"Excellent." He raised an eyebrow. "And your feet?"

She gave him a mock scowl. "Just fine, now that they have rested."

Laughing, Willem turned to greet Lord Einhard who was on his way over to join them. "Good morning, my lord."

"Good morning, Willem, Margarethe." He seated himself beside his niece.

At that moment the servitors brought in the meal—great golden loaves of bread and mugs of cider. After the blessing, they broke off chunks of the bread and began to eat, each apparently waiting for the other to speak first.

"Willem, not long ago I asked you to write some music for May Day—for a certain occasion," Lord Einhard began.

Willem listened quietly, wondering what Margarethe might be thinking.

"We have not spoken of it since, but the assignment is yours, if you are still willing."

"I am willing, my lord," Willem said reluctantly. "But it would help with the composition of the piece if I were to know what choice your niece has made."

Lord Einhard glanced at her. "Margarethe knows that she is at liberty to discuss the matter with you as soon as she has made her decision. She also knows," he said, frowning a little sternly, "that time is running out, and she must decide soon. Naturally, she will talk with the man himself before she discusses her plans with any of us."

Willem nodded respectfully. "Of course, though I suspect she was dancing with him just last night."

Margarethe shrugged as if disgusted with the whole business. "Naturally—since I had to dance with each of the brothers, which is tedious indeed to keep track of so many. I may make my choice known soon just to be free of the accounting!"

Einhard chuckled, and Willem forced a smile. "About the commission for the music—I will double the amount I originally told you, Willem, since you are no longer in my employ."

"Thank you, my lord. I will do my best," he said, a lump forming in his throat.

Lord Einhard leaned over the table. "I know how difficult this is for you, and I appreciate it all the more," he said holding Willem's gaze. "I wish things could be different."

Willem sensed the man's sincerity and wondered at it. Did he not consider Gregor a worthy man for his niece? Or did he favor Willem for some reason? Surely Margarethe could come to love Gregor as other women had come to love their husbands in arranged marriages. It was he—Willem—who would have no wife, no love, ever. His memories of Margarethe would have to last him a lifetime.

He could find no reply for Lord Einhard and ducked his head to consider the spicy liquid in his mug. Just then, he felt a small hand under the table, reaching for his. She gave it a brief squeeze before releasing it. He dared a quick glance in her direction and saw the tears starring her eyes. How could he bear it?

They ate in silence before Margarethe spoke up. "How long will you help with the war, Uncle?"

"I will stay with my troops for another week at least. Then, if all goes well, I will leave them with Otto and go home next Lord's Day. I'm sure Mechthild is anxious."

"As any wife would be, Uncle."

Willem heard the slight catch in Margarethe's voice, and knew she was dreaming of how it would be if it were she, sending Willem off to war.

"Is your patient doing well?"

"Much better, Uncle—now that we have found that she loves music as much as we do."

"Have you asked what instrument she plays? It is likely that she has talent. Her mother was quite musical, as I recall."

"Hilda has not spoken of her mother, but Albert told me she died last year of a fever. Did you know her, Uncle Einhard?"

He nodded. "She was a noblewoman, a younger daughter for whom no husband was found. She pleaded with her father to let her marry the miller, and he was persuaded to do so. It was a love match, as I understand it, and they were very happy together." Lord Einhard grew pensive, then excused himself from the table and left the hall.

Willem watched him go, then looked at Margarethe, who was gazing sadly at him. "Why do you suppose he told us that story?"

She shook her head. "I don't think he meant to tell it. I doubt that he even realized how it would affect us until afterward."

Willem sighed deeply. "I am a nobleman, but I would be better off if I were only a commoner. . .one with a mill."

"Perhaps you can find one at a good price and buy it," she teased, then bit her lip as he gazed at her, his longing written all over his face. "I'm sorry, Willem. So sorry," she whispered. This habit of jesting when in pain—he couldn't remember if he had acquired it from her, or she from him.

"I would make a poor miller," he said, going along for her sake. "Perhaps I could buy a pig farm instead. I could spend my days making music and hire a pig herder to do the work. Would you be available for the job?"

Her mouth dropped open, but her eyes were sparkling—more like the old Greta. "Me? Highly unlikely."

Gregor, who was approaching from behind Margarethe and had overheard her last remark, dropped down beside her. "And just what is highly unlikely, Margarethe?"

"Willem here fancies himself a pig farmer, with me as his hired hand. Can you imagine it?"

Gregor joined in their game. "Willem, you've always had a rare gift for searching out a person's talents. Still, I would never have thought of Margarethe as a pig herder until you suggested it. But now I can see it quite clearly."

"Well, I have no pigs as yet, and I have bathed. So why does no one sit beside me?" He threw up his hands. "Even Lord Einhard has left us."

"Speaking of Lord Einhard, he told me something interesting yesterday," Gregor said, turning to Margarethe. "He said that you have decided not to marry one of his other allies, but one of the four brothers of Beroburg. Is that true?"

"It is true. I desire a good mother-in-law, and the others could not promise me anyone so kind as Lady Edeltraud. So I will do what I must."

Gregor's face lit up. "Excellent! You will make me a fine sister-in-law."

Willem watched the disbelief spreading across Margarethe's face. "Sister-in-law?"

Gregor gave Willem a conspiratorial wink. "Klaus will be so pleased. He has wanted to marry you and tame you since you put that frog in his shoe."

"That poor frog," she shuddered, in an attempt at lightheartedness. "But it is not Klaus I will wed. He needs a wife with a very good sense of humor—and much more patience than I."

"He does, indeed," Gregor agreed, nodding vigorously.

Seeing the direction of this conversation, Willem decided to withdraw. "I have work to do," he said, rising. "And it is best that I get to it. If you or your patient should like some music this afternoon, Lady Margarethe, send for me. I'll be in my study."

"Thank you, Willem," she said. The love and longing in her eyes pierced him through, but there was nothing he could do about it.

❧

Hilda was disappointed when she discovered that she had slept through morning Mass. At home, she never missed a service on the Lord's Day. Still, she did feel rested, and for that she was grateful. Jolan, too, had overslept in the adjoining room and emerged sometime around mid-morning, yawning and rubbing her eyes.

"Good morning, Jolan," she said, realizing her error almost at once. "Oh, forgive me. I meant to say, *Lady* Jolan."

"No matter, Hilda. I would be happy if we forgot about using titles altogether. It is only an accident of birth, after all, that you were born in a village and I was born in a castle. Now, shall I help you to the privy?"

"Oh, I've already taken care of that. I'm feeling ever so much stronger today."

"It is the rest and the healing herbs, I think. Wait here," Jolan instructed her, "and I'll see about breakfast."

But she only went as far as the door. "See what someone has left for us? Our breakfast. Whoever it could be is taking very good care of you."

"Yes. . .He is," Hilda agreed, thinking how gracious was God to send her such loving new friends.

They broke their fast together, eating in silence. Then Jolan helped her dress, and Hilda braided Jolan's hair in return.

"Is there anything you would like to do today, Hilda?"

"I need to write to my father. He will have the news from

Lord Albert, but he would much prefer to hear from me. That is, if there is paper I can use."

"I'm sure there's some in the music room, though Willem always uses parchment for writing music, because it is easier to erase."

"The music room?"

"Yes. Instruments and music and such are kept there. It is an inner room, fairly safe from the damp. Would you like to see it?"

"I would love to see it—and all the instruments, too."

They left the chamber and walked toward the music room, surprising Willem there as they pushed the heavy door open. He was sitting on a stool at a cluttered table, plucking a lute. He turned at their entrance, and Hilda could see that he had been crying—a very strange sight indeed, for she had been taught that men, once they are grown, never cry.

Without thinking, she went to him and put her arms around him. He put the lute down and returned her embrace ever so gently.

As they drew apart, Hilda saw that Jolan was looking on in amazement. "Willem, what is it? What's the matter?"

"It's all right, Jolan. A small matter."

Jolan stared at him curiously for a bit, then turned to Hilda. "There is paper here for your letter. Do you want to bring some back to our chamber?"

"Or you may use this table if you wish," Willem said, clearing a place for her at the table.

Jolan seized upon the notion. "A fine idea, Willem. You can stay here, Hilda, and write while I make some infusions in the infirmary."

"Very well," Hilda agreed, taking the chair Willem held for her.

When Jolan had left the room, Hilda spoke what was on her mind. "Now it is my turn to listen. If you should want to talk, Willem, I am here," she offered.

Willem sat very still, saying nothing, gazing at the blank parchment before him.

"If you will not, or cannot tell me what is troubling you, then I will simply pray that the Father of us all, who knows all things, will give you whatever it is you are praying for."

She was a little surprised to see the tears welling again in his eyes—so much so that they began to trickle down his cheeks like a spring rain. She covered his hand with hers and set about to beseech the Heavenly Father to comfort Willem, that good man.

"Thank you, Maid Hilda. You are most kind," he whispered. "I must say, though, that I seldom weep this way—and certainly not before an audience."

She smiled. "And don't I understand tears? I've shed enough of them in the past few days. I've heard that God stores every one of them because He knows our pain."

Without another word, she began to write, only half-hearing the melody he was picking out while she worked. Almost unconsciously, she began to hum along. And when Willem joined in, taking the lead, she switched to an alto harmony, their voices blending flawlessly.

When she looked up from her writing, the look on his face startled her. "Oh, I've taken liberties, I know! Would you forgive me?"

"Oh, it isn't that. Not at all. It's just that I was surprised to hear your harmonizing. If that tune were a song, would you prefer that it be a chorus or a verse?"

"Verse," she said with great conviction. "The melody line of the verse needs to be simple so that the words will be prominent. The words of the chorus will be remembered for their many repetitions." She paused. "But who am I to tell you such things. You're the musician."

"No more than you, it seems, Maid Hilda." He appeared

strangely moved. "What else do you know of music?"

"I can sing a little—when my ribs are not cracked—and I can play rebec, shawm, and recorder, the instruments I had as a girl."

"Your mother taught you," he stated, surprising her.

"How did you know?"

"Lord Einhard spoke of her at breakfast." He looked very sad again, probably because he feared bringing up such a painful subject.

"Lord Einhard knew her long ago, before she married my father."

"I see." Willem nodded but did not pursue the matter further. "Do you have any ideas about the chorus?"

"Have you a recorder here? My ribs hurt me when I sing."

Willem passed her a soprano recorder.

"Thank you. Now what words have you given the chorus?"

"I haven't written the chorus yet. My head and my heart are working at cross purposes today."

Hilda paused to pray silently, then played the tune of the verse again before launching into something else entirely—a melody that carried the essence of the verse, but was bold and triumphant and proud.

Willem stared at her, transfixed. "Can you play that again?"

She nodded and obeyed, noticing that Willem was paying close attention. He picked out the tune on his lute, looking to her for approval, then transcribed the music while Hilda finished her letter.

"Hilda, this may not be the music I should be writing today, but it is a worthy tune. If it earns me a commission, part of it is yours," he said, looking perfectly serious.

"Oh, no, Willem. I couldn't take anything. Mine was only a small idea. You had already done the important work. Besides, I have no need of money." There was no way she could ever save up enough to replace her lost dowry anyway—money lost to the physicians her father had secured for her mother, against all hope.

At that moment there came a tapping on the doorframe, though the door was standing ajar. Looking up, she saw that it was Albert. "Greetings," he called out to her. "I was told I might find you here."

"Greetings, my lord," she said, pleased to see him again.

"Hilda has been most helpful with a composition I was working on," Willem told him.

"The lady loves music. I'm looking forward to hearing her sing when her rib has healed."

Gazing at the two men looming over her, Hilda felt her throat begin to close and a suffocating feeling overtook her. While she wanted to flee, her knees buckled beneath her when she tried to stand, and she put her hand to her head to ease the dizziness. Her heart, pounding wildly, felt as if it would leap from her chest.

Albert pulled up a chair and sat down near Hilda, saying nothing.

"What's wrong?" Willem wanted to know.

Albert shook his head, frowned, and whispered, "Play something soft and soothing."

Willem obliged, and Albert held out his hand to her. As the music flowed through the room, her pulse gradually ceased its rapid fluttering, and her breathing slowed. Closing her eyes, she held tight to Albert's hand.

"What happened, Hilda?" Willem asked gently when the lovely piece came to an end, and she had regained her composure. "What frightened you so?"

"I really can't say. I suppose it's just that I suddenly became aware that I was alone in the company of two men. It makes no sense, for I count you both friends." She sat very still, pondering the problem and clinging to Albert's hand.

"I understand," he said. "I've had such fears when facing

battle—or worse yet, recalling the horrors of past battles. It's as if some darkness overtook my spirit for a time."

"That's it exactly! Do you often have these sensations at night as well?"

"They're worse at night than at any other time. But they won't last forever." She could tell he was trying to comfort her. "As the experience dims, so will the night terrors."

She thought Albert looked very tired, as if he were remembering something even now.

"I, too, have had nightmares, frightening dreams that I cannot remember when I awake," Willem added.

"You have company, I see," said Jolan from the doorway.

Albert smiled. "Come join us. Hilda needs some hugs."

Jolan laughed as she entered the room and put her arms around Hilda. "I have not had enough hugs since I left home myself," she said. "They're good medicine—like music," she said, catching Willem's eye.

"Oh, Hilda," said Albert, "before I forget why I came here, I must tell you that I will be leaving after dinner today. I want to go home to see how my people are faring before I return to the battlefield tomorrow. I can take a letter to your father if you wish."

"I have only to seal it." How thoughtful Albert was, she thought, always anticipating her needs before she asked.

"And since it is two hours until dinnertime and my armor is cleaned and polished, I have nothing further to do. I was hoping to find a chess partner."

"Music is better than chess," Hilda suggested, looking at Willem and Jolan in turn.

Willem frowned. "I have a composition to write."

"It's the Lord's Day, Willem. Write it tomorrow," Jolan said with a saucy toss of her head.

"Very well. Let us have music then."

Jolan was pleased. "I'll go fetch Margarethe."

Hilda thought she saw another wave of pain cross Willem's face at these words. Was Margarethe the cause of his tears earlier? She decided to pray the more earnestly for both of her new friends.

≥≈

Where the time flew Hilda could not say. But after Margarethe joined them and they took their instruments to the hall to play, the moments took flight with the wings of a dove. It was all so delightful—choosing and carrying the melody without stopping between songs, until all the music blended in one harmonious whole. At a nod of the head, someone new picked up the lead and started another tune. With the beautiful sounds enhanced by the high and vaulted ceilings, the hall began to fill with eager listeners.

By dinnertime, Hilda was quite tired, but happy. Still, seeing her begin to sag, Albert appeared concerned, and she wasn't surprised to hear him say, "You three continue without us. I'll take Hilda upstairs."

She did not protest when Albert picked her up at the bottom of the stairs. "Thank you, my lord. I will be strong again soon, I hope, and will no longer be a burden to you."

"You are no burden at all, Hilda."

Was this how it was with these people? Always tender and compassionate toward others? Or was there some special bond that linked her with this man—the man who had rescued her on the most terrible day of her life?

eleven

After dinner Margarethe rode with Gregor as she had promised. She wore her favorite riding habit to help ease her nervousness and concentrated on enjoying the sun on her face and the spring breeze scented with the perfume of hyacinths and lily of the valley.

The shadow of a cloud slid across the fields as they cantered down the hill; it moved slowly, but could not be halted. Margarethe was reminded of May Day's inevitable approach and that she was doing something today to smooth its way.

She and Gregor spoke of many things. Family traditions. Favorite pastimes. The war. Now, better informed, Margarethe found herself in complete sympathy with Lord Otto. "I thought his war was only about land. I never realized how much more was involved. I'm ashamed that I have never prayed for victory for you."

"It isn't too late to begin," he teased her.

"And so I have, good sir."

"Good. I hope you also pray for my safety."

Margarethe thought about that. "Are you ever in real danger?" she asked. "As a captain in full armor, I would think you are much safer than one of the foot soldiers or archers."

"True," he conceded. "But war is still a bloody business, and anything can happen. I covet your prayers, my lady."

Margarethe glanced over at him. He looked so strong, as if nothing could ever harm him. "I will pray," she promised. His smile was quick and contagious, and she found herself smiling back.

They followed the main road for a furlong, then Gregor

suggested that they take the forest path. It was cooler here, and Margarethe was glad for her warm cloak. They stopped in a glade ringed with daffodils.

She looked around, delighted. "How lovely," she breathed.

"I thought you would like it." His eyes were for her alone, she noticed, not for the flowers nor the lush forest foliage. She had always been comfortable with Gregor. If she felt awkward now, it was only because of the serious subject they must explore together.

"Gregor, you know you can speak the truth with me, don't you?"

"I would hope so. It's not as if we haven't known each other since we were children."

"This morning you said I would make you a good sister-in-law. . ." She stopped, her courage wafting away as on a sudden breeze.

"You would, indeed," he said, nudging his horse next to hers.

She sighed. "Gregor, must you put me through this humiliation?"

"I think you are doing very well. Do go on." He appeared to be enjoying this little game.

She shook her head. "I must know the truth about the proposal you sent my uncle two years ago."

"Three."

"Very well, then, three years ago. I know it would not be honorable for you to withdraw it if you changed your mind—"

"Not to mention expensive," he interrupted. "When Ludwig withdrew his proposal, he had to give gifts to both your father and your uncle."

"Neither of them shared those gifts with me," she pouted, and Gregor laughed at her comical expression. "Three years is a very long time, and I want to know if you still wish to marry me—if you ever did. Perhaps it was your father who made you send the proposal."

Gregor nodded. "I must admit it was originally my father's idea. But that was back when I was a lad and before you were all grown up. Now, it's very much *my* idea." He took the reins from her hand and began leading them deeper into the forest.

"Father began talking about one of us marrying you when he first met you as a child of seven. Through the years, other young ladies were considered, of course, but you were the only one I ever wanted to be my wife."

She smiled at him through a veil of tears and took a deep breath. "Well, since you would probably make a poor brother-in-law, and I do have to marry one of you, I was wondering if you still wanted—"

In the shadows, she could not read Gregor's face as he dismounted and strode over to her. But she could see that he was quite intent as he lifted his arms for her. She slid off her horse and he held her, searching her eyes.

"We are always jesting, you and I, Margarethe. But I truly believe we can bring much happiness to each other. Will you marry me?"

She stood gazing up at him, breathless. The moment she had dreaded was upon her. There was nothing else she could do. "Yes, Gregor, I will," she whispered.

He pulled her into his arms and held her tight. She tried desperately to hold back the tears, but to no avail. Poor Gregor. He was kind and gallant and deserved so much more than she could offer him. But there was room in her heart for only one. Willem. Always Willem. . .

Gregor pulled away to study her face. "What's this? Tears? And this our betrothal day? I *much* prefer your laughter."

He held her closer, and she leaned into him, steadying herself, surprised to find that she was enjoying his warmth. She felt a stab of guilt. What kind of person was she, and how could she go through with this farce?

He kissed her forehead and stood back to let her look at him while he spoke of serious matters. "I won't rush you into marriage, Margarethe. But I would like your kisses in greeting and farewell. Do you think you could manage that?"

Striving for a casual tone, she cocked her head. "So your brothers will remember whose I am?"

"Something like that. But I am quite proud that you have chosen me, Margarethe. I admire you greatly."

"I admire you, too, Gregor. I always have."

He smiled mischievously, and Margarethe was instantly on her guard. "It occurs to me that if we will be kissing publicly, perhaps we should practice privately, don't you agree?"

She looked up for a moment, pretending to consider. "Very well," she said and stood on tiptoe to brush her lips against his.

He laughed, caught her to him, and kissed her soundly. It was pleasant enough—something like kissing Jolan or Uncle Einhard or Aunt Mechthild. Nothing like the all-too-brief kisses she had shared with Willem that had only left her wanting more.

Gregor seemed disappointed and a little anxious. "I can see that we will have to practice often until we get it right."

She smiled as he gave her a leg up to remount, hardly necessary since her horse was small and her legs were long. On the way back, they spoke of Gregor's holdings and his castle. They talked of possible wedding dates, what to wear, whom to invite. They spoke of many things, but they did not speak of love.

The cloud shadows moved faster and faster across the fields until, pelted by large raindrops, Margarethe and Gregor were forced to gallop for home.

෪

In the hall, Willem worked on the lyric for the music he and Hilda had composed. Feeling the need to be near people rather than closeted away in the music room, he had come here where there was always a bustle of activity—pages scurrying about on some errand, kitchen maids preparing the tables for a meal, and an occasional visitor passing through on an inspection of the castle.

His musical partners of the morning had scattered. Lord Albert had left after dinner, Hilda was abed, Jolan was nowhere to be seen and Margarethe was out riding somewhere with Gregor.

Truly, his writing was not going well. The music was more suitable for battle than a betrothal—a betrothal, he felt sure, which was being arranged this very afternoon. Just one step nearer to the time when his love would be lost to him forever. He had to think of something cheerful, or there would be no songs of any kind this day.

Hilda had surprised him with the wild exuberance of the chorus she had been inspired to write. Perhaps it had been born of her recent ordeal—something far worse than anything he had experienced. He studied the blank piece of parchment and thought about her rescue, her faith. The concept would make a worthy song, though the attack itself could never be set to music. It was far too terrible. Still, there might be some way to use its message.

He was absorbed in the process when Margarethe and Gregor entered the hall. At the sound of their voices, he looked up from his writing and met her eye briefly before she glanced away. Then she and Gregor walked toward his parents' solar.

Willem picked up his writing materials and went back to the music room. Solitude was better than staying here to witness what would surely come next.

In the music room, Willem prayed for Margarethe—the prayer he had covenanted with her to pray, though each day it seemed the answer was more remote than the day before.

"It's me, Lord. Willem. Father, You know my heart. You know that I desire Margarethe as my wife more than anything on earth. And You know which of us would be the better husband for her. Please help me. Teach me how to pray for her. Help me to desire Your will more than mine.

"I could also use some help with my music—the music you gave me and Hilda. As for Hilda, Lord, I ask that she would grow strong in body, mind, and spirit. Hear her prayers and reunite her with her father. Lord, since she may have trouble finding a husband after being dishonored, I ask You to send her a good and loving man who will not hold it against her." He continued on, praying for all those he cared about, even Gregor—the man who stood between him and the love of his life.

&

At supper, there was wine at every table, a most exceptional occurrence since the retainers usually had only ale or cider to drink. Some of the soldiers took the opportunity to drink too much and became inebriated before the final course was served. Willem was tempted, but stayed with one cup.

Against his will, his gaze kept straying to the head table, where Margarethe and Gregor were chatting and laughing together. They seemed quite happy and content. Even Lord Einhard and Lord Otto were in an unusually jovial mood, considering the fact that they would be heading back to the battlefield on the morrow. Only Klaus looked somber and morose.

As soon as the last course was cleared, someone in the crowd called for music, and Willem gathered the ensemble for the first set and began. People were in a festive mood tonight, which only served to heighten his despair. Attempting to rid himself of his melancholy, he chose lively tunes and called on Jolan to help him.

When Margarethe beckoned, he strolled over, strumming

his lute as he went. "Yes, my lady?"

"You can count on me for my share of the music, Willem," she said. "I would be happy to play or sing."

"As would I," Gregor put in. "I know the baritone parts to all the old songs."

Willem was struck with a sudden inspiration. "I will call on you soon. Your lady, also."

He noticed Margarethe's grimace at hearing the term. Gregor, on the other hand, beamed with pride.

As it turned out, when the time came for some new songs, it was the four of them singing in a quartet that drew the heartiest applause. Following that performance, Willem wisely changed the mix, using Jolan on small drums and Margarethe on lute. She and Gregor sang an old comic duet that featured an argument between a husband and wife. The sketch was always hilarious even when done poorly. But tonight, with the talent and personality of the actors, it was a great success.

After a short instrumental interlude, someone called for Margarethe's love song. There was no way around it. To decline would be to invite rumor and speculation. And so Willem called Margarethe over and whispered, "Can we do this?"

"Have you stopped believing that God answers prayer?" she retorted.

His doubts fell away as he read the determination in her eyes. "Lead on, my lady." They sang as well or better than ever, and he was cheered by the reception the song received.

When the time seemed right for some silliness, Willem made a great show of selecting a special group of singers— Lord Gregor, Lord Einhard, Lord Klaus, Lord Gottfried— Gottfried rolled his eyes, knowing that it had to be a joke—Lord Ludwig, and Lord Otto. "And I, of course, shall be a part of this carefully chosen chorus." There was a ripple of approval and a few cheers.

With great deliberation, Willem went to each man and whispered the name of a song in his ear. At his cue, each one began to sing a different song. The crowd realized what had happened a second before the men did, and roared with laughter. Willem knew it was a trick that would work only once, but it had been worth it to see the reaction all around. As the laughter began to subside, Willem closed with a worshipful number that ended the evening on a high and holy note.

It was quite late, and many had already drifted off to bed, when Willem found Hilda sitting in the back of the hall. "Have you enjoyed the evening, Maid Hilda?"

"Yes, Willem, thank you. You are not only a master musician, but excellent with people."

He was impressed again with her cultured speech, recalling that this was not some simple village maid, but of of noble birth through her mother. In addition, he was pleased with her compliment. "I do enjoy making merry, and I try not to offend while doing it. Are you getting tired?"

She nodded. "I think I shall retire now, but I can walk on my own."

"That won't be necessary when I'm around." He scooped her up, carried her up the stairs, and set her down in Jolan's chamber.

"Thank you, good sir." She stood, gazing up at him expectantly.

"You are most welcome, my lady," he said. He studied her for a moment longer, then, "Earlier today you said you would pray that my prayers would be answered."

"Yes, Willem."

"I hope you intend to keep your pledge."

"Of course I will, for I know you must have something important on your mind."

"Very important. The Scriptures tell us to pray in faith, but some days my faith is weak, and I have need of a strong friend."

She smiled. "I prayed today for you."

"And just in time, too," Willem said. "Of a truth, my lot has been bleak of late, but your words give me courage, even though the situation still looks impossible."

"God is good with impossible things. Remember the man born blind? No one had ever healed someone who was blind from birth, but Jesus did."

"I will remember. Good night, Maid Hilda, and thank you for your counsel."

He left the room and as he descended the stairs, he murmured to himself, "I have much to be thankful for indeed. I was not born blind. My only problem is that I was born *second*—to a man with little land."

ও

Remembering all that had happened, Margarethe had difficulty falling asleep. Even her dreams were fragments of the day's events. Gregor's proposal, his kiss. Lord Otto and Lady Edeltraud's joy when they heard the news—a joy that would be for naught if, by some miracle, her continual prayer were answered.

Nor could she forget the look on Willem's face when they came into the hall. His pain was so visible, so raw. It was all she could do not to tell Gregor it was all a mistake and run to Willem on the spot. No matter the consequences, no matter what she had promised her uncle.

She recalled the clever staging Willem had contrived with the evening's music, especially the bit with the singing lords. How was it that he was able to make people laugh even when his own heart was breaking? Margarethe cried herself to sleep.

She woke, frightened, from a dream she could not remember. Her face was wet with tears. Afraid to sleep lest the dream return, she lay still for some time. Then she rose and dressed herself in a woolen tunic and surcoat. It was too dark to tell what colors she had chosen. And her hair was likely a mess, so she put on a cap and tucked her braids underneath.

She left her chamber quietly and walked toward the chapel. She would surely be the only one there at this hour, so long before dawn. But when she arrived, she was surprised to find the chapel packed with fighting men. She would have withdrawn except for a man near the door who saw her and made room for her. As Mass had just begun, she stayed.

Margarethe looked around the chapel until she spotted Gregor, then gave her attention to the ritual and prayed along with the priest.

Afterward she waited by the door for Gregor. He came looking for her, and seeing her, put out both hands in greeting. "I am touched that you came. I didn't realize that you knew about this early Mass for the fighting men."

"Oh, I didn't know, but couldn't sleep and needed to pray."

"Well, I'm glad you're here. We will be leaving after we break fast. Would you keep me company until then?"

She smiled and nodded, and they made their way to the banquet hall, where the servants were already placing baskets of bread and mugs of ale on the tables. Gregor led her to the head table, where they sat down with the other captains. Looking out over the vast hall, she saw all those young and vulnerable faces, so very different from the men who had laughed and sung and shouted the night before.

"Just before going off to battle, they are quiet," Gregor began. "They're wondering who will come home again and who will be buried on the field of battle."

She looked at him as if she'd never seen him before. How different their worlds. And how necessary the life he led to the security and comfort of hers. She took in Gregor's clothing— quilted breeches and aketon with a chain mail mail hauberk and the surcoat embroidered with the family crest—and felt apprehensive. "You do wear plate armor, don't you?"

"Yes, but not until we reach the battlefield. As you may imagine, it's quite awkward and uncomfortable."

"I am beginning to understand that this war is real and not just a fanciful tale for storytellers and minstrels," she said, feeling an unaccustomed pang of fear.

Gregor covered her hand with his. Again, she noticed the scars marring the bronzed skin. Fearing for him, she clung to his hand all the way to the gathering place on the grounds outside the hall.

At this hour of the morning, it was still cold, and she shivered in the predawn chill. Gregor put his arm around her and drew her close while a squire brought out his war horse, prancing and neighing, the stallion's breath pluming in the frosty air. The great beast stamped his feet as if eager to be off.

When it was time to mount up, Gregor hugged Margarethe close. "God be with you," he whispered.

"And with you, Gregor. I shall be praying for you, for all of you. Do not allow yourself to be injured, or you will have to answer to me."

He gazed down at her for a moment longer, then bent to kiss her. She returned his kiss willingly. She had promised, after all.

Gregor swung into his saddle and, with one last little salute, rode to the front of his battalion. Lord Otto and Uncle Einhard were already mounted, waving their swords to signal the call to move out.

She watched, with a sinking heart, as the men trotted their horses through the gate. They would be gathering more troops from allies along the way.

With no trace of dawn tinting the sky, Margarethe felt smothered by the oppressive darkness. She would never love Gregor with her whole heart—as she did Willem—but she could not bear to see him marching into certain peril.

twelve

Willem was surprised to find Margarethe in the hall when he came from Mass. When she explained that she had stumbled onto the soldiers' worship service by accident, he nodded. "It is the custom here, I've learned."

"Willem, we should not be seen together in front of Lord Otto's people. I do want to talk with you, though. Would you have time to visit with me later today?"

How could he resist her? "It seems I'm giving voice lessons to nearly everyone in the castle these days, but I will always have time for you, Greta."

The familiar nickname came without thinking, and he noted her pleased smile. "I am not overly busy with my patient, so if you need help with some of your lessons, I'm available."

"An excellent idea, my lady. I may take advantage of your kind offer."

She left him with a nod and made her way to the head table to join Lady Edeltraud. Willem could not take his eyes off her. He wondered at her choice of clothing today. He had never seen anyone wearing a green surcoat over a blue tunic. The effect was startling.

His thoughts were diverted by a group of his students who joined him at the table, broke bread with him, and made conversation. He assigned lesson times for each of them, and then asked if anyone would like to receive instruction from Margarethe. Two of the women were enthusiastic about the idea.

The afternoon passed pleasantly enough. Willem worked

on Hilda's story, changing it so that she was rescued just before the assault, and making it vague enough that there could be no disgrace to her. He used no names, of course, but the people close to her would recognize the story.

The music lessons went well, and Willem introduced the two women to Margarethe, who put them through a series of exercises. After the women had left, Willem and Margarethe sat together in the chamber—much like her study chamber at home. They were alone, but only until the next student arrived, which should be any time now.

Apparently Margarethe was feeling more and more uncertain about her betrothal, and voiced as much to Willem. He listened to her fears and misgivings, trying to ignore his own pain. "Truly you are in a worse position than I, for I need not pretend to love anyone else."

Margarethe's eyes filled with tears. "I am pretending nothing, Willem. How can you say that?"

"I have seen you with Gregor. Either you really do care for him, or I have taught you more of acting than I meant to."

"Of course I care for him," she said a bit defensively. "Gregor is a decent man, and I will treat him decently."

"Does that include kissing?"

"I believe it is expected of betrothed couples."

He could see the pain in her eyes, but pressed on. "So. I see. And do you enjoy kissing him?"

To his surprise, Margarethe grinned. "Indeed, I do. Kissing Gregor is much like kissing my aunt!"

Willem laughed with her for a moment, then grew serious again. "Forgive me, *Liebchen,* for suggesting that you would be dishonest with Gregor. But I wonder what you would say if he asked you about me."

He could see that she was studying on the matter before replying. "I will not lie to him, but neither will I tell him anything he does not ask."

She hung her head and looked so sad and small, Willem wanted to take her in his arms and comfort her. He satisfied himself with holding her hand instead. "I know you for an honorable woman, Greta. This must be very hard for you."

She did not answer but sat very still. After a time she said softly, "Willem, should not people who are betrothed speak of love? I have said nothing of love to Gregor, and he has said nothing of love to me."

&

On Friday Hilda persuaded Jolan and Margarethe to wash her hair. It was a delicate operation since they had to remove the bandage beneath her cap and take pains not to disturb the injured area on the back of her head.

While Hilda's long golden blond hair was drying, Margarethe asked the others to pray with her for the men on the field of battle. "The three of us can accomplish so much more than one," she said. "Remember Christ's words? Father Bernard has told me that our Lord said, 'If two of you shall agree on earth as touching any thing that they shall ask, it shall be done for them of my Father which is in heaven'?"

The others readily agreed, each one having someone dear to her who was facing danger. Each in turn prayed for all that was on her heart. When it was Margarethe's turn, she gave thanks for these women who were sharing their lives so willingly.

But something Hilda had said stirred her curiosity. The maiden had asked God to bless Willem and to answer his prayer. What prayer? Could it be that he had confided in Hilda? Surely he would not betray their love!

&

On Saturday night the men came home, loud and boisterous once more. Margarethe dutifully sought out Gregor out and kissed him. "You might do well to have a bath, my lord," she suggested, pinching her nostrils shut with one hand

"I can see that you will be one of those wives who is always giving orders," he teased.

"And I can see that you will be one of those husbands who needs much instruction," she countered, smiling. "There is plenty of hot water, and singing as well. Your mother tells me that's a combination you can't resist."

"My mother is right, as always." With a jaunty wave, he headed off for the bathing area. "When you see me next, you won't recognize me," he called over his shoulder.

Margarethe listened to the rowdy singing coming from behind the curtains in the portion of the hall assigned to the bathers. Willem's voice was unmistakable, and soon she could hear Gregor joining in. Then Willem dropped out, and a moment later she could hear him say, "You're wounded!"

Gregor's answer was muted, but she caught the mention of her name, followed by a round of laughter and a voice Margarethe did not recognize. "Ewald's captains he does not fear, but Lady Margarethe is another matter."

She was relieved. It must not be a serious injury. She went to the page who was guarding the entrance to the bathing area and announced, more loudly than necessary, "Please ask Lord Gregor to meet me in the infirmary when he is finished."

"Yes, my lady," said the page, and the laughter behind the curtains resumed.

Margarethe found the infirmary quite busy when she arrived. The place was filled with soldiers—none of them seriously injured—with Jolan and some other women mixing herbs and making poultices.

"While you're waiting, you could roll that linen material into bandages," her cousin suggested.

Margarethe finished one roll and set about straining some fresh infusions. Then, feeling someone watching her from the doorway, she looked up. "So there you are, Gregor. Are you badly hurt?"

He shrugged. "It's only a scratch. I had your prayers protecting me, didn't I?"

She nodded, but gathered up an armful of ointments and bandages anyway. "Come. There's no room here to treat you. We'll have to find another chamber."

She led the way to the solar. "Where is your wound?" she asked when they were behind closed doors.

He removed his tunic and showed her a nasty-looking scrape, surrounded by a purpling bruise on his side. Bringing a candle closer, she inspected the injury.

"Judging from these marks, I'd say this was made by chain mail." She looked Gregor in the eye. "How did you get this?"

"From a lance belonging to one of Ewald's captains."

"Were you wearing your breastplate?"

He ducked his head sheepishly. "Not at the time. You see, that plate was made for me three or four years ago, and I've outgrown it. So I left it off just this once."

Margarethe found herself trembling. "A lance goes through chain mail like a flame through paper. Had that captain a better aim—"

"His aim was true, but his horse slipped," Gregor explained. "The fellow was most disappointed. As for me—well, I was lucky."

Margarethe drew in a sudden breath. "When did this happen?"

"Yesterday, about midmorning."

She felt the sting of sudden tears. "It was not luck, Gregor. It was the hand of God. Some angel tripped that horse. Jolan and Hilda and I were praying for you at that very moment." She began to cry, and Gregor gathered her into his arms.

"Then keep on praying, my lady," he whispered as he held her. "Your prayers are more powerful than the enemy's weapons."

Eventually she moved out of his arms and got to work,

using soothing ointments and wrapping his ribs with strips of linen. "No broken bones, at least," she said. "We can thank God for that."

"And I must thank the other ladies who prayed for me. Jolan, did you say, and Hilda? Is she the woman Albert brought in from the village?"

"Yes. She seems like one of the family already." Margarethe tied off the bandage and gave Gregor a final pat.

"God is so good. In my prayers I have been thanking Him for you," he said shyly.

She was stricken with guilt. "Oh, Gregor, I don't deserve your praise," she said, thinking of her deception.

"Whose idea was it to pray yesterday?" he interrupted.

"Mine," she whispered.

He gazed at her steadily. "God used you to save my life. Even if something happens and we never wed—" she felt an icy premonition—"I will be grateful that you were in my life long enough to save it."

❧

It was good to be at morning Mass on this Lord's Day, Hilda thought with satisfaction. She thanked God for her continuing recovery. She rejoiced that the life of Margarethe's betrothed had been spared. It proved to her that God had been listening when they prayed, which gave her hope that her own personal petitions would be answered as well.

Lord Albert, who had also attended Mass, met her on the way out. "Are you planning to break fast in the hall today?"

She nodded, feeling her cheeks heat beneath his curious gaze.

"Then let's go over together."

They walked in companionable silence to the hall and Albert seated her, then surprised her by sitting across from her at the trestle table. "I go home after dinner today, Maid Hilda. Will you have another letter for your father?"

"I've started one to tell him of our answered prayer on behalf of Lord Gregor."

"Gregor told me about that last night. He also said that he had an appointment with the armorer today, Lord's Day or no, to have his breastplate altered. On Margarethe's orders."

Hilda laughed. "Margarethe will see to that. And you were right to believe that she would choose Gregor over the rest of you."

Albert speared a chunk of bread with his knife. "We're all relieved that she has finally made her choice. She and Gregor are suited to one another, and it frees the rest of us to look for other life companions."

Hilda's puzzlement must have been plain to see, for Albert went on to explain. "Each of us proposed to Margarethe, and none of us could seek other wives until she decided. Ludwig got out of it by gifting Lord Einhard and Margarethe's father handsomely."

"Did she know you were waiting to hear from her?"

He shrugged. "Most men would disregard any proposal that is not answered within six months. But we were truly hoping she would consent to join our family. So, other than Ludwig, we chose to do the honorable thing."

They spoke of lighter matters as they ate, then Albert escorted Hilda to the music room, where he left her to finish her letter to her father.

Later on, Hilda climbed the stairs—somewhat slowly and painfully—and went to Jolan's chamber where she played a rebec until Albert came. She stood to greet him.

"Your father will be glad to hear from you. He misses you, but wanted me to assure you that you have his blessing to remain here until you have completely recovered."

She was comforted. "I do feel at home here at Beroburg. Everyone has been so kind to me."

He stood gazing down at her for a long moment. "Would

you pray for me? I feel the need before I take my leave."

Gladly she stepped up to him, took both his hands in hers, and prayed, asking for his safety first of all, then for wisdom and victory and for his future happiness. When she was finished, Albert added his own prayer for her, including a request for her future husband—that God would prepare him for her.

He concluded his prayer, then smiled down at her. "I do hope you don't mind my imploring the Almighty for your future husband. But for all I know, you might be planning to join the sisters at the monastery."

"That isn't my calling," she assured him.

Suddenly, however, the awful incident of a few days past, rushed over her like a tidal wave, threatening to engulf her, and she felt Albert's arms catching her before she slipped, unconscious, to the rush-strewn floor.

❧

In Margarethe's chamber at Adlerschloss, Lady Mechthild waited by the window commanding the best view of the road. She was hoping Einhard would be home today. And when she saw a lone rider in their colors approaching, she left the chamber and went to her own to check her appearance in the mirror. She was wearing her husband's favorite ensemble—a scarlet surcoat over a slate tunic. Her braids were coiled over her ears, and it was warm enough to do without a head covering. Still, just in case, she got out her scarlet cloak and carried it with her.

In the hall outside her door, she found Sir Johan polishing his armor yet again and greeted him. "I think Lord Einhard is on the way. I spied him from the window."

"That's good news indeed, my lady. I shall look forward to hearing about the battle and joining the rest of the troops soon."

"You must be anxious to do just that. Is your ankle well?"

"As well as can be—thanks to the skill of your healer, my lady."

Mechthild smiled. This young knight had as yet seen no battle as a knight, only as a squire. And like all the gallant young men, he was eager to be a part of a cause greater than himself.

She started out of the hall, donning her cloak as she went, then walked briskly to the stable, knowing it would be Einhard's first stop. She was not disappointed.

He had already dismounted by the time she arrived and greeted her with a hug.

"Oh, Einhard, I'm so glad to have you back safe and sound," she said, offering a silent prayer of thanks. "What news do you bring?"

Summoning a page to take his things to the donjon, he walked with one arm around his wife. "For one thing, our niece has chosen her husband at last."

"Gregor?"

He nodded. "Just as we predicted."

"Does Margarethe seem happy with her decision?"

"Well—" he faltered. "She is trying. She rose very early this morning to attend the fighting men's Mass, then came out to the field to see him off. She seems to care about his welfare."

"Oh, that's a good sign. I do hope she can get over Willem quickly and make a good life with Gregor."

She noticed that Einhard was thoughtful for a long moment, and wondered.

"I'm still sorry about that. Margarethe and Willem should be wed. They're so right for each other."

She looked over at him with a coy smile. "Einhard, ours was an arranged marriage, and we have been very happy together, haven't we?"

He squeezed her hand. "But neither of us was in love with

anyone else. Margarethe and Willem truly love each other, the way you and I love each other. Perhaps she will learn to love Gregor, but I fear she'll never be as happy as she would have been with Willem."

She could not answer, or she would weep. And it wouldn't do for her people to see their lady's tears and wonder what had caused them.

&

Inspired to write another verse for the battle song, Willem went to the music room immediately after dinner. It did not take him long to get his thoughts down on parchment and then to shape them into verse. "Thank You, Lord, for helping me. I know it serves some purpose of Yours."

He read the verse over again and was satisfied. It told of a captain saved from certain death by an angel sent in answer to the prayers of the women at home. Willem reflected on a truth he was just grasping. A battle can be won or lost by the actions of people who are nowhere near the battlefield.

And now he had an idea for the chorus. Still, he must speak with some of the soldiers who had seen battle and could give first-hand reports.

With two verses and the melody of the chorus written and driven by the need to complete his project, Willem carried paper and pen with him and went back to the hall to see who might be about.

There he found Gottfried talking with two knights and asked if he might join them.

"Of course, and welcome." Gottfried moved over on a bench to make room for him. Seeing the supplies in Willem's hand, he asked, "What have you there?"

"I've been working on a song, and I want to include some heroic tales from this war. I was hoping you might tell of some exploit that should be remembered so that I might put it in the song for all to hear."

"A worthy project, indeed, Willem. Have you met Sir Osgood and Sir Johan?"

Willem nodded. "Sir Osgood I've seen about the castle, and Sir Johan I recall from Lord Einhard's house. Have you just joined us?"

"Yes," said the younger knight. "The healer finally said my ankle was well enough for me to fight and I've been most eager to perform some heroic deeds of my own." The other men laughed and clapped him on the back.

"Much of war is mud and blood, I fear," admitted Gottfried. "Heroic deeds are sung about because they are so rare."

Far into the night, the two knights talked, recounting their adventures on the field of battle and others they had heard told around the fire. Willem scribed furiously. And when everyone else had left the hall and the two knights had retired at last, Willem was still writing.

thirteen

On his next foray into the village, Albert stopped by the mill and spoke at length with Karl, an interesting man, all the more so for being Hilda's father.

"My lord, will you marry?" the miller asked over a mug of mulled cider.

"It is expected of me. And so I shall."

"Have you chosen your wife?" Karl scratched his chin, dusty from the grain he had been grinding.

Albert shrugged and shifted uncomfortably on his hard stool. "My father has put several choices before each of us. I'm not particularly valuable for making alliances, since I am but the youngest son. But perhaps I can help solidify some alliance we've already made."

There was a long silence while both men gazed into the fire, pondering their own thoughts. Then the miller let out a sigh. "It is sad that nobles must marry for politics and not for love."

Albert set his mug down and wiped his mouth. "Oh, I have some say in the matter. In fact, since Margarethe made her choice known, I have been praying more than ever that the Lord would show me the wife He would choose for me."

"And I'm persuaded that He will. Take your brother's escape from the lance. 'Twas an amazing thing," said the miller, his eyes wide with the memory of the tale. "And I know that my Adelie—God rest her soul—was an answer to my prayers for a good wife. For not a finer woman ever lived—unless it would be our Hilda." His face, beneath its coating of flour, flushed scarlet. " 'Tis a hard thing to forgive the man who stole her virtue—"

A log blazed higher, sending a spark spiraling out onto the wooden floor. Albert rose to grind it out beneath his heel, then turned to regard the miller with compassion. "Be at peace. I happen to know that your daughter has already forgiven him and is making a good recovery from her ordeal. The physical scars have almost healed and, with the help of the Almighty, she will be able to put the whole sordid business out of her mind and heart. In fact—" he gazed off into space, remembering their prayer before they parted— "I am truly impressed with the goodness of her spirit."

Karl smiled, his chest swelling with obvious pride. "It is because of her mother. My wife was of the nobility, you know—and a godly woman. She taught the girl well."

"Yes." Albert turned again to peer into the fire, watching the flames dance, as if they were responding to some unseen wind. "Yes," he said again, thinking, reflecting. "She is quite a remarkable young woman—your Hilda."

❧

Willem was utterly distracted. Whatever he was about— whether coaching a vocal student or strumming his lute in the privacy of his own chamber—the song would not let him go. It plucked at his heartstrings with a relentless will of its own. Even when he tried to pray for Margarethe, the words came, unbidden, to his mind: "Write the song. Write the song." Not the betrothal music he'd been commissioned to write, but another. A song of such force that it took his breath away.

❧

By midweek, when Margarethe and Hilda examined Jolan, instructing her to breathe deeply, they were convinced that her rib had healed sufficiently to permit her to sing.

She was ecstatic. "How can I thank you? I have had the best healers in Bavaria!"

"And now we'll see just what kind of voice you have," Margarethe said. "We've been needing a third person for a trio."

Hilda laughed with delight. "So that was your motive then. You thought to mend me so as to put me to work! But I must warn you—I didn't inherit my mother's warm, rich alto voice."

They were soon humming together, finding Hilda's range and proclaiming her to be a low soprano. Before long, they were harmonizing on a song Jolan and Margarethe had sung for Hilda many times during her convalescence.

At the end of the second time through, they were startled by the sound of clapping coming from the open doorway and turned to find Willem standing there. He was looking most handsome this morning, Margarethe thought with a catch in her heart—dressed in the blue that so enhanced the blue of his eyes.

"Wunderbar!" Those eyes were twinkling now. "Well, Maid Hilda," he said, "I'm happy to see that you've progressed in your recovery—and that we have a fine new attraction for our after-dinner entertainment."

Margarethe sensed his delight, knew that discovering new talent was a great adventure for him.

"Perhaps—if you would excuse us, Lady Jolan—" Willem gave his most courtly bow— "Margarethe and I might have some time with Maid Hilda to explore her gift a bit more."

Jolan waved her hand. "Oh, I have work to do." She lifted a volume—*Causae et Curae*—from the table. "I must copy some passages for the infirmary, so I should be busy all afternoon. But if you need me later for any reason—"

"Such as the three of you helping with some music for the end of the week?" Willem asked.

Margarethe cast a doubtful glance in Hilda's direction. It might be too soon for the injured maiden to be facing a roomful of people. But her fears were quickly allayed.

"I've sung at village fairs and in our church with my mother," Hilda explained with a reassuring smile. "I should welcome an opportunity to repay all of you—and my host and hostess—for their kindness to me."

Willem lifted her hand and kissed it. "Dear lady, I hope you plan to stay for a very long time. You are sorely needed here."

Knowing the gesture meant nothing, Margarethe felt only a small pang, soon replaced by the exhilaration of watching Willem at work.

In the music room, the afternoon sped by as he put Hilda through a series of vocal exercises, making notes, and pointing out areas of strength and weakness. While she sang, Margarethe wandered about the room, finding some parchments on the table that looked interesting. There were verses about heroic deeds, written in a style unlike anything she had seen. Another contained some music, scrawled hastily—a verse and a chorus. She had picked up the parchment to study it more carefully when Willem caught her in the act.

"And what do you think, Greta?" he said softly, having left Hilda to stand in front of a mirror to practice some scales.

Margarethe smiled sheepishly. "I think you are writing something of great importance—such wonderful tales— though I can't imagine what the occasion would be."

"Nor do I." He shrugged. "I only know that when I pray a certain prayer, these words pop into my head: 'Write the song.' And I know that it is this song."

"Will you hum the tune? I couldn't make it out over the background music in the room."

By this time Hilda had joined them at the writing table. "What song is this you speak of?"

"You'll recognize the chorus," Willem said, moving the page so she could read over his shoulder. "You gave it to me when I had nothing but the verse."

She seemed surprised. "You would want to use that chorus?"

"If you'll agree. But I shall give you credit."

"Indeed you will not. I gave it freely. Besides, it is not mine anyway, for it came after prayer—when you mentioned to me that you needed an idea."

Margarethe, who had been listening intently, was struck with wonder. "Then *God* is writing this song."

Willem nodded in agreement. "It seems so." He moved to pick up his lute. "I'll sing what has come to us so far."

He sang the verse about Gregor's miraculous delivery from death on the battlefield, then hummed the melody to the chorus.

Margarethe clasped her hands together when he had finished. "It's magnificent, Willem! Truly inspiring. We'll pray that the words to the chorus will be revealed to you."

"God will send them when He is ready." Willem set the lute on the table and dropped onto a stool with a long sigh. "It is the music your Uncle Einhard commissioned that concerns me now. I'm not sure why it won't come." She saw that he could not meet her gaze.

Margarethe felt her own heart sinking at the thought. "But it will be needed in less than a month. Surely you have at least started it."

"That's just the trouble. I had started it when this music came and consumed my mind entirely. I'm not sure what to do."

"Forgive me," Hilda put in. "But may I ask what music you're speaking of?"

"Lady Margarethe's uncle has asked me to compose a song for the announcement of her betrothal on May Day," Willem answered, with an uncharacteristic note of bitterness in his voice.

"Oh. Is that what you meant when you told me you had to compose a score, but that your mind and heart were at cross purposes?" Hilda asked gently.

Margarethe held her breath, waiting for Willem's reply. "I do not want to see her wed. She would move to Gregor's castle, and I will miss her. . .music."

It was enough. Hilda need not hear the whole truth. But when Margarethe saw the tears gathering in Willem's eyes as he put the music away, she read what his lips had not uttered—and must never utter again.

&

On the evening before the Lord's Day, the newly formed trio performed in not one, but four songs. Willem was hugely pleased with the response of the hall and with the expertise of the performers. Truly he was blessed to have such singers in the castle—and such friends.

Willem watched Hilda closely throughout the evening. She seemed to be recovering well from her injuries. She tired before her companions, but otherwise seemed much better. Still, at times it seemed that her body was present while her spirit was elsewhere. Willem prayed for her, knowing that more healing must come before she was fully restored.

"It is your turn to sing again, Sir Willem," called someone in the crowd. And with that ridiculous application of a knight's title, he laughed, then obliged them with a song.

At the evening's end, Willem looked for Gregor in the hallway outside his chamber—the first time he had been able to catch the man without Margarethe at his side all day. "I would have a word with you before you retire."

Gregor frowned. "Shall we return to the hall?"

"No, my lord. I'd prefer we talk undisturbed. This is a private matter," he said, feeling a growing apprehension.

"In my chamber, then." Gregor jerked his head toward the door.

Willem walked in with him and surveyed the room as Gregor uncovered two cluttered stools where they could perch. Surely Margarethe had never seen this room, Willem thought, or she would already be lecturing him about housekeeping.

"What is on your mind, my friend?" Gregor asked.

"It is this war. I find myself very much in sympathy with the cause, and I want to help." Willem watched Gregor's eyebrows rise and made himself sit still while the knight contemplated.

"You help us already, Willem. You can't imagine how refreshing it is to come home to music and laughter and dancing. The atmosphere of this place has improved sevenfold since you came."

"Thank you, my lord. I trained to be a knight, but since there was no war, I have never seen battle."

"Are you saying you wish to fight with us?"

"I am."

Gregor dropped his gaze and studied the toe of his boot, propped against the table leg. "How long since you were in training?"

"Six years."

"Much has changed in weaponry and strategy in the last six years. You don't own armor or a war horse, and being a foot is too dangerous for any nobleman." He narrowed his gaze. "How is your archery?"

"I am. . .*was* deadly accurate," Willem replied. Was there no way he could prove himself?

Gregor appraised him with a sweeping glance. "You're strong, there is no doubt of that. Perhaps you could still string a bow."

"I would be proud to do so," he replied, his spirits falling. He *needed* to go to the field as a knight. It was knights who did the great deeds. It was knights who were sometimes rewarded for their acts of courage.

Gregor's expression was grave. "Willem, I am pleased that you want to help. And I am honored that you came to me to offer your services. But I cannot allow you to fight in any capacity in my battalion. You're too valuable to risk. Men like me are expendable, but a man who can bring an entire castle joy simply by opening his mouth, cannot be replaced."

"Would it not be my own life I'd be risking?" he pled. "Have I no choice?"

"My father needs you to hold the household together. The depression has lifted since you came to us. And your life is not your own. You're a believer, bought by the blood of Jesus Christ. As your Supreme Commander, it is He who gives the orders."

Convicted, Willem fell silent. "I had not even thought to pray about this," he confessed. "I must do what He calls me to do."

"There is another reason I cannot let you fight in my battalion," Gregor continued, speaking with soft intensity. "If something happened to you, Margarethe's sorrow would overwhelm her. She loves you so." Willem froze in his seat, not believing his ears. "It's true. You're her closest friend, and I could not bear to see her hurt."

After another lengthy silence, Willem sighed. "Then I will do what I can without fighting. Some are called to fight, and some are called to sing."

"I would gladly trade you callings, my friend."

Gregor rose to see Willem out, and cuffed him lightly on the shoulder as he bade him farewell.

That night Willem could not sleep at all. His prayers were filled with thoughts of Margarethe. "Write the song," came the familiar response.

"How can I write of what I do not know, Lord?" Willem groaned. As he waited for the answer, an idea dawned—like the rising of the sun."

❧

Margarethe was up before first light and attended the fighting men's Mass as she had once before. Gregor seemed to be expecting her, and had saved her a seat. He was becoming so affectionate and considerate that her guilt increased each time she saw him.

During the stillness of communion, she prayed, "Father, please help me find a way out. I don't want to hurt Gregor, but I feel I belong to Willem. Only You can bring order to this chaos, and I humbly ask You to do it."

After Mass, she walked beside Gregor, turning only when she heard Willem's voice calling out. "My lord, I could not sleep for an idea that will not leave me alone."

"Willem," Gregor said sternly, "I gave you my answer."

"It is not what we talked about—yet it is," Willem began. "Shall I tell you in front of your lady, or will you turn aside for a moment?" He was short of breath, and his eyes were dancing with excitement.

Margarethe stared until Willem noticed her, but he quickly looked away. What could he be thinking of? She questioned his sanity, so strange was his manner as well as his attire, for he wore traveling clothes.

"Margarethe, I will join you when I can," Gregor said, dismissing her.

Once again Willem caught her eye and glanced toward the ceiling. From that gesture—their private signal—she knew he was imploring her to pray. But for what?

Help, Willem, Lord. Give him Your wisdom. Let him know what path he is to take. He seems so desperate of late. Comfort him. Let him know that I love him still. I do not know what he is scheming with Gregor, but if the idea is from You, then please bring it to pass.

She continued to pray as she went to break her fast. At the table, she sat and waited for the men to come in, nodding to some who drifted in from other parts of the castle.

When Willem and Gregor entered the hall, she could see their heightened enthusiasm, which only increased her apprehension. What was even more curious was that they headed directly for the main table, but passed her by on their way to speak to Lord Otto. She could not overhear the exchange that was made, but from the back-slapping that followed, she could only assume they were well pleased with something.

"Stay, Willem, and sit with us," Gregor invited when he

had left his father and returned to Margarethe.

To her surprise, Willem remained, dropping into the seat to her left while Gregor took the right.

"What is happening?" she asked, glancing from one to the other.

"Meet our new camp minstrel, my lady," Gregor said with a broad smile.

At first she could not make out what he was telling her. But when understanding came, she smiled. "It is well, Willem. You will find the missing words for the chorus there." She fought the thickness forming in her throat.

"Then you do not mind?" He stopped suddenly and tipped his head to one side, an eyebrow raised.

"What? Mind leading the evening music and teaching all your voice lessons?" she said with mock indignation, trying her best to hold back the tears. "My lord," she said, turning to Gregor, "I know this bandit is paid for teaching. Will you let him treat me so?"

Gregor laughed. "Indeed. Teaching will keep you out of mischief while I'm away." He dropped his voice. "We need him, Margarethe. Morale is low in the field, and he can encourage us with his music. Do as you please with the students. But you will be serving us well if you can keep the people happy at home."

She nodded miserably and applied herself to her bread and cheese. When it was time for the men to go, they rose. A feeling of near panic threatened to cut off Margarethe's breathing.

"It is a wet morning, my lady," Gregor said. "I'll bid you farewell here."

She stood on tiptoe to kiss his cheek, and he drew her to him to whisper in her ear. "Willem could use a hug as well. He was concerned about leaving you with all his work."

She faced Gregor as he released her, then turned to embrace Willem. "God be with you—and keep you from harm."

fourteen

For the next few days, Margarethe was completely occupied with teaching and coordinating the nightly music. All of the students were pleased that they would not have to be without instruction while Willem was away. But as for all other matters pertaining to the music of the house, she was careful to consult with those who had shared the chief musician's post before his arrival. They seemed pleased to have been consulted—equally pleased to be free of the responsibility.

Margarethe had never known a house so fond of music. On previous visits, she had assumed that the rich musical variety offered after supper was in honor of the guests. Not so. Here at Beroburg, musicians were used regularly, with jugglers and acrobats simply offering a diversion while the singers rested between sets.

So preoccupied was Margarethe, in fact, that it was Thursday before she noticed Hilda's silent withdrawal from the routine activities. Concerned, Margarethe began to look for her.

Not finding her anywhere about, she went to Hilda's new chamber adjoining her own. Finding the door ajar, she stepped in. Hilda was standing at the window, gripping the cold stone sill with a white hand.

"Hilda? Greetings. I've been missing you in the hall—"

When the maid turned, Margarethe could see that her eyes were red and swollen "What is it? What's wrong?"

Hilda shook her head. "I hope it is nothing. But I've been calculating the dates. . ." She sighed deeply, then dropped her gaze, unable to meet Margarethe's eye. "My monthly blood is late."

Margarethe caught her breath at the implication, but fought for composure—for Hilda's sake. Rushing over, she took her friend's hand. "Women are sometimes late for no reason."

"I have *never* been late."

"But I've heard that when a woman has had a serious injury, it is not unusual for her whole body to react to the pain. . . ."

"No, Margarethe," Hilda continued sadly. "I was not severely injured in body. But now I'm so very frightened—" she sobbed, and fell into Margarethe's arms where they wept together.

❧

With orders to remain at base camp with the cooks and other servants during the daytime hours, Willem used the hours to finish his song. Sitting cross-legged in the tent he shared with Sir Johan and his squire, he peered out into the misty rain, praying and thinking.

The words for the chorus came to him the first day out. But when they began to formulate themselves in his mind, he waited, resisting the urge to record them at once. Drawing aside, he prayed, needing to be sure that they were divinely inspired. At the same time, he was consumed with a sense of urgency to complete the song.

On the third day in the field, the battle took a bad turn. The men came in discouraged, and fights broke out among some of the foot soldiers. The rain that had been falling when they left Beroburg was now relentless, pounding against the tops of the tents, the dampness seeping into everything. The bedrolls were soggy, water was standing in puddles inside, and there was not a thread of dry clothing among them. Supper was late because the bread was ruined, and the cooks had to send runners to Lord Albert's castle for more.

In the midst of all this, Willem walked among the men, attempting to spread a little cheer. But for the most part, they turned a deaf ear.

If ever there was a time for a rousing song, this was it. Still, Willem wanted to be sure and knelt in a corner of his tent to pray. The longer he prayed, the more he was certain that this was the night to introduce the new music.

After their meager supper, the men grew restless, and at Lord Gregor's direction, Willem stepped to the front. "A song!" someone cried. "Give us a song!"

"And high time, I'd say," called another.

Thus encouraged, Willem gathered his lute, stood in the entry of the main tent, and struck the first chord. One by one, he led them in some of the old familiar songs that had been favorites at the castle. He could feel the tension draining away.

Finally, when he had their full attention, he spoke. "I have a new song this night. I cannot take full credit for writing it, for most of it came to me only after much prayer. This song is about you, and it is a gift to you from the Lord God."

Willem strummed the opening chords, whispering a prayer as he did, "Here it is, Lord. Use it as You will." He sang the first verse to utter silence. During the chorus—that wild and proud sound, accompanying words of love and courage—there was a stirring among the men. The second verse was received much like the first, with rapt concentration. By the fourth chorus, the men had risen to their feet and were clapping in time to the music. Hearing a voice join his, he turned to find Lord Albert harmonizing.

Even so, at the song's conclusion, Willem was not completely prepared for the response. The men cheered heartily and threw their hats into the air. There was a general stampede as some clapped comrades on the back or shouted their approval. He himself was mobbed by the lords, and his lute was whisked away somewhere.

"*Wunderbar,* Willem! Exactly what we needed!"

"How did you gather all those stories? It must have taken months."

"Well done, Willem. Is there a baritone harmony you can teach me for the chorus?" That, from Lord Gregor.

Soon their conversation was interrupted by a widespread chant: *"Wieder,* Willem, *wieder. Wieder,* Willem, *wieder!"* they shouted. "Again, Willem, sing it again!"

Gregor escorted Willem back to the tent entry, and the squire who had taken his lute into the tent to keep it dry, returned it to him. A cheer went up as he positioned his lute.

"It's a very long song," he called above the din of rain and raves. "Are you sure you want the whole thing?"

"The whole thing! Don't leave out a note!" came the enthusiastic reply.

They were of one accord, except for one ruddy-faced fellow, who yelled, "How about adding more about women?"

A roar of laughter went up—a good sign indeed. Surely this was the song he was meant to write, for it was hitting the mark—much like an arrow, aimed true, striking the heart of its target.

So Willem sang the entire song again. This time, he was joined on the chorus until an entire male choir was ringing through the night:

> To trade and travel freely,
>   No tyrant taking aught;
> Our families safe, our farms secure—
>   This is what we've sought.
>
> Maidens, wives and mothers
>   Doing battle on their knees—
> Praying as they work all day;
>   God has heard their pleas.
> Partners with us in the conflict—
>   Mighty without sword;
> We fight for freedom, heart to heart,
>   Contending for the Lord.

Inspired by their example,
    We have a sacred trust.
And so we have the courage
    To do all that we must.

Though there were calls for more, Willem backed off, yielding the floor to Lord Otto, who led in a prayer for victory—something that had never happened in their history, to anyone's recollection. But on the way back to their tents for the night, it was the melody of Willem's new song they were humming.

On Friday, a messenger arrived from the battlefield with news of a great change among the troops.

Lady Edeltraud summoned Margarethe and Jolan to the solar. "Perhaps the two of you can help me make sense of this. Remember how rainy it was the first four days of the week?"

"Yes, Aunt," Jolan replied.

"All the men were wet and miserable and deeply despondent. Then Willem sang a new song, and suddenly the black mood lifted." Lady Edeltraud rose, pacing the room. "Now I know the messenger to be a sober young fellow, but he vows this is the best song he has ever heard. Everyone is singing it as they go about their business, and praying as well.

"Even Otto has been leading the men in prayer." Edeltraud's eyes were huge. "On Thursday our men gained ground—a significant amount, I understand, and today the enemy retreated entirely." She peered into the two faces. "Tell me, if you know—how could a song bring such a change?"

There was a slight pause while Margarethe searched for the right words. "It is not the song, Lady Edeltraud, but the God who gave the song that made the difference. We, too, need to pray."

"Yes, yes, I can see that. I pray this victory will continue in spite of Ewald's reserves. Oh, and that is something else I learned from the messenger." Margarethe waited expectantly. "The extra soldiers came from Austria, as we suspected. Ewald gave a daughter in marriage to an Austrian lord in exchange for troops for this season."

"What does his daughter think of that?" Margarethe wondered aloud.

Lady Edeltraud sighed. "I do not know. I know only that I could never trade a child of mine to win a battle."

❧

Friday evening Willem and Gregor talked by the blazing fire outside their tents. "Never have we had a musician stir us as you have, Willem. My father wants to reward you at the end of the campaign. Think now. What reward would you have?"

Willem shrugged. "What does every man want?"

Gregor surprised him by laughing. "The one thing my father has more of than any man in Bavaria—land."

Willem nodded, gazing into the fire. "And if I had that which every man wants, my life would still be empty, for it would come too late."

"Too late? How could land come too late?" Gregor asked.

Willem turned a sober look on him before he glanced away. "Forgive me, Lord Gregor. I talk too much."

A heavy silence descended between them before Gregor cleared his throat. "Willem, let us sing a song, just us two. Do you know 'The Lady in Blue'?"

Oh, yes. And in green, and brown, and scarlet. She was lovely in purple as well. "I do."

They sang softly so as not to disturb anyone, their voices blending.

As the fire died down, Gregor clapped Willem on the shoulder and went off to his bedroll. But Willem sat, watching the dying embers, and allowed his tears to fall.

❧

After getting ready for supper at the end of the week,

Margarethe stopped in to see Hilda. "How are you?"

"The same." Tears welled in the blue eyes. "Except that I grow more fearful each day."

"God will be with you—and Jolan and I will stand by to help. I'm sorry my new duties have called me away so much, and I could not be with you more."

"It is well. Jolan has with me, and singing helps." Hilda looked so hopeless that Margarethe felt a rush of grief for her friend. At least the men would be home tomorrow night. Hilda seemed happiest when Albert and Willem were near.

"Perhaps tomorrow we will be able to hear the new song that has so stirred the fighting men," Margarethe suggested, hoping to distract Hilda's gloomy thoughts.

But it was not to be. "I'm so ashamed to see them. Especially Lord Albert. How will I tell him about. . .my problem?"

"You have nothing to be ashamed of. But do you need to say anything? You are not even certain yet."

"Perhaps not. But he will have only to look at my face to know there is something amiss."

It was true. Hilda's usually rosy cheeks were pale, and her eyes were puffy from weeping. "Still, he has made himself your protector. He may know a way to help you."

Hilda shook her head. "Some things cannot be helped. I am praying that I am not with child, that it is something else instead. But if I am—"

Margarethe sat with her, holding her hand, and thought about the situation. What a tragedy. The poor thing had already suffered cruel abuse. Now she might be called upon to bear pity and humiliation as well. Not to mention the suspicions of the village folk. She had hidden herself away at the castle and had not returned to her home since the attack. An unmarried woman with a child would have a sad life, even the daughter of the miller, a man of some means.

The very best thing would be for Hilda to marry immediately

so that the child would be assumed to be her husband's. Else she might be shunned for life. At the very least, tongues would wag.

Still, Hilda was not betrothed and had no prospects o of marriage. Nor did she have a dowry, what with her mother's long illness taking all their money. And even if Margarethe's uncle was willing to provide a suitable dowry, she was almost sure the proud Hilda would never accept it.

Margarethe stirred, pressing her friend's hand before she rose. "I must go. Will you come down to supper?"

Hilda sighed and followed her out the door. "My appetite is poor. But I will come. Perhaps the change will do me good."

❧

Margarethe's was the first face Willem spied when he arrived at the castle with the troops, more joyful than usual after a report from a scout had revealed that the enemy had fled the fighting field.

"I've heard about your new song and am anxious to hear it," she said, her smile warming him—heart and soul.

"Then you shall—most likely this very night," he said, feeling his love for her shining through his weariness. "How went this week for you?"

"Your students and the music kept me very busy. I'll tell you all about it when you have the leisure to listen."

"I will seek you out when I do—after a good hot bath." He stood, admiring her for a moment. "It was a good week, a necessary week, but I missed you," he said softly, hoping that Lord Gregor wouldn't come along to spoil this moment.

But it was Lord Albert who passed by with a little wave and a salute. "Willem," she whispered urgently after Albert had moved on, "pray for Hilda. She needs us so."

❧

Just as Willem left for the bathing area, Gregor came in. Margarethe greeted him with a kiss as he had requested, grateful that both men were home safe once again. How very strange it felt to love one man with all her heart, the other with only half.

She heard the news from the front, rejoiced with Gregor, then saw Albert rush down the stairs, take his mother aside and go with her to speak with his father. Lord Otto frowned, then the three of them walked out of the hall together. *Father,* Margarethe prayed silently, *if this has something to do with Hilda, please work Your way in it all.*

Jolan caught her eye across the room and gestured for her. Margarethe obeyed, seeing that her cousin was surrounded by fighting men, fresh from their bath, claiming to need massages even though they had not been wounded.

The men, who had been clamoring for her services, dropped back at Albert's approach. "Cousins," he said, "I need your prayers, though I cannot explain why just now."

"Is it something to do with our friend?" Margarethe asked.

He nodded.

"You can count on us, Cousin," Jolan assured him. "We have nothing pressing to do here, anyway." Her glance swept the group of men who were clustered nearby, waiting for the conversation to end.

"Then I can proceed with courage."

"And where are you going, Albert?" asked Margarethe.

"To the home of Karl, the miller," he called over his shoulder as he strode away and disappeared through the door.

The miller! she thought. *Hilda's father!*

৯৯

Willem was accustomed to good treatment in this household, but now he was treated with the respect accorded a great hero. At supper, he was given a place of honor at the lord's table, and afterward, a cry went up for "the song."

He looked about and caught Margarethe's eye, then rose and accepted the lute one of the other musicians handed him.

Without introduction, he began the song, his heart swelling as a group of the soldiers joined him on the chorus, filling the hall with the glorious sound.

At the end of the song a great cheer went up, and Willem felt the joy he saw radiating from Margarethe's face. It was well. She was pleased—more than pleased.

Lady Edeltraud rose from her seat and came to see Willem. "I did not understand all the fuss about a mere song. But now that I've heard it for myself, I can see how one song could inspire men's hearts and put an end to war."

Willem bowed low over her hand. "Thank you, my lady. But I believe God is the composer of that song."

"I believe it, too. And I pray He continues to use it."

If he received any more acclaim, Willem thought to himself, he would have to pray against that deadly sin—pride!

☙

Hilda stayed in the hall long enough to hear the stunning song everyone was talking about. Her eyes filled with tears at the sheer beauty of it. She recognized her story, of course, and was happy for Lord Albert, who had been made a hero forever through his part in the song.

But now she was wondering how he was faring with her father—and what their business might be. Feeling the need to visit the garderobe, she did not remain for the rest of the music, but climbed the stairs for the small chamber down the hall.

She was inside only a short time and emerged, flushed with happiness and relief. Her feet fairly flew down the steps on her way to share the good news with her friends.

Then she went back upstairs to give thanks to God and to await Lord Albert's return. For whatever he was arranging for her would now be for naught.

fifteen

Margarethe was doing a ring dance with a group of ladies when someone tapped her on the shoulder. She turned to find Hilda, wreathed in smiles, with Albert and his parents. They all looked so happy that she withdrew from the dance to learn what had happened. Hilda offered a hug instead of an explanation while Albert left to fetch Jolan.

At the back of the hall, he launched into an announcement. "We've splendid news! It appears that we have discovered a solution to Hilda's dilemma."

Margarethe and Jolan exchanged bewildered glances.

"You're both aware of the. . .uh. . .the difficulty Maid Hilda has been experiencing." At their nods, Albert continued. "Well, my first thought was that she must marry immediately."

Jolan shook her head. "We thought of that as well, But it's impractical, of course, since she is not even betrothed. Besides—" Where was all this leading? Hadn't Hilda confided that the grievous assault had not left her with child?

Albert grinned. "Yes, now—thanks be to God—there is no need to rush into a marriage for the purpose of saving her honor." Well, so now Albert knew as well, Margarethe thought.

"In spite of all that, however, the lady has consented to marry a man of whom she has grown quite fond."

Margarethe watched, astonished, as Albert leaned over to plant a kiss on Hilda's cheek.

"So there is to be another wedding in this house," Lord Otto said, with Lady Edeltraud on his arm, smiling proudly.

Margarethe could only gape as Jolan let out a little squeal

and threw out her arms to both Albert and Hilda. Then Margarethe collected herself. "I am so happy for you both," she told her friend. Yet even as she kissed Albert's cheek, she thought of Willem. Such happiness would never be theirs.

≥≈

Willem looked on as the little tableau at the back of the hall unfolded. Still, he had not an inkling of what was going on until the radiant couple approached. "Willem, Hilda and I are to wed."

Willem covered his surprise by drawing them both into an embrace. "My heartiest congratulations, Lord Albert, Maid Hilda." Then, he inclined his head toward Hilda. "I must say you've a job ahead of you, taming this one." Hilda made a face, but clung to Albert's arm.

Had Margarethe known all along? Is this what she'd had in mind when she'd asked him to pray for Hilda? How strange—that a lord could marry a miller's daughter, when a nobleman could not marry a lady simply because he had no land.

≥≈

In spite of a sleepless night, Willem rose early on the Lord's Day and attended Mass. Toward morning his thinking had cleared, and he realized that a miracle could still occur for himself and Margarethe. She was betrothed to another, but that was not the same as being wed, and the betrothal had not yet been made official—with May Day still a fortnight away.

If Margarethe broke it off after that, it would be an insult to Gregor. Insulting the knight was not something Willem cared to do. He had not intended to like the fellow, but now that they were friends, he felt an unexpected loyalty.

Hilda joined him at table. "Forgive me, Willem, but you seem sad today. How can this be when God has given you such a wonderful song to encourage the men? Why, you're a hero!"

He shook his head mournfully. "I am no hero. I'm a failure."

"A failure?" Her eyes grew round. "You are so gifted and talented, and everyone loves you." He made no answer, but sat watching the servitors bring in the meal. "Does it have something to do with this prayer you have been praying?" she asked.

He gave her his full attention and nodded. "The prayer that has *not* been answered."

She tapped the table with a fingernail, pondering. "You have never shared with me the nature of your prayer, but did God not instruct you to write a song when you prayed?"

"Yes. And I obeyed."

"Then surely the answer to this prayer is on the way. Can you not see? It is something like going to a bazaar to purchase something from a merchant. At his booth, you choose some cloth. The merchant tells you how many coins, and you lay them on the counter. After all that, would you then walk away without the cloth?"

"Of course not."

She gave a little smile. "There, you have it. You should be thanking the merchant and picking up your purchase. Do you not think that our Lord is much like that merchant, and you— the buyer?" She eyed him expectantly, and Willem blinked in amazement.

"That is a weighty matter," he said, clearing his throat. "I will have to give it some thought."

At that moment Jolan and Margarethe joined them. "Are you planning to purchase some cloth, Willem?" Jolan asked.

He felt the beginning of a blush. "Not likely." Then he changed the subject. Looking about, he saw none of Lord Otto's family. "Where are all the lords?"

"They are meeting in the solar," Margarethe replied.

She was lovely today in light blue and purple, a combination she favored.

"For what purpose?"

She shrugged. "Gregor was secretive. Did Albert mention anything to you?" she asked Hilda.

"Nothing."

"I need to talk with you today, Willem," Margarethe began, "about your students and the music for this week. Jolan, you should come, too, for you've had your share of students."

Willem bowed. "I shall be ready whenever you need me, my lady—in the music room."

He quickly finished eating and excused himself. In the music chamber, he took up his lute. There he strummed as he considered what Hilda had said. The maiden made good sense. The answer might well be on the way.

Thanking God for that which had not yet come, Willem hummed a tune he heard in his mind, then plucked the strings, feeling his way through the song. Before it slipped away, he reached for parchment to seize the moment. The Lord continued to surprise him at every turn. Maybe Maid Hilda was right, after all. . .

&

"A messenger, my lady, with a letter from the Schwarzwald," announced a page, interrupting the music lesson Margarethe was giving.

Offering no explanation, she excused herself and dashed down the stairs. She had seen her parents only twice in the nine years she had been a member of her uncle's household, and news from home was dear. In fact, because of the danger on the roads, they had all been advised against traveling and so it had been several years since she had seen them.

With trembling fingers, she took the letter the messenger handed her, unsealed it, and read:

Our dear Greta,
 Too much time has passed since last we were

together. And now we learn that our little one—only a babe yesterday, it seems—is to wed.

With the improved roads and the battle far to the south, we are told that travel to Oberburg is safe, and we long to help you celebrate your betrothal at the feast on May Day.

Until we meet again,
Papa and Mutti

Margarethe wiped a tear with the back of her hand. Would that her parents were coming for a visit only—and not to celebrate the beginning of her lifelong imprisonment—a marriage she dreaded with all of her heart.

❧

It was late on Lord's Day Eve when the fighting men returned, more boisterous than ever. Margarethe ran down the stairs with Jolan and looked for someone who could tell them what was happening.

"Willem!" she called, spotting him among the men. "What is the news?"

"It was a complete rout. Ewald's men turned tail, and Lord Otto gave chase. The front has been pushed all the way to his castle," he said, grinning. "I rode along when I heard. It was glorious! I may have to add another verse to the song."

Jolan grimaced in a comical expression. "I hope I never have to learn that long song."

"Oh, Willem, is it almost over?" Margarethe asked.

"Very likely. The scouts from the south reported that many of Ewald's hired Austrian troops did not stop at the castle, but kept going toward home."

Someone sent out a cry for a healer, and Jolan responded, leaving Margarethe and Willem alone. "My parents will be here soon," she said, suddenly feeling awkward.

His gaze pinned her to the spot, and she felt as if she could not draw her next breath. "I know you will be glad to see them."

"Yes—but. . .oh, Willem, why did it have to end this way?"

Glancing about to be sure they were not being observed, he leaned close to her ear and whispered, "Remember, our God can do anything. Never give up hope."

Gregor came in just then and enveloped her in a hug. "Sweet Greta, how goes the battle at home?"

"We are still praying, Gregor." She looked around for Willem, half expecting him to be gone. But he stood there, grinning.

"Did Willem tell you why we are so late tonight?"

"Yes, and it is good news indeed. Do you think the war may be over before Midsummer?"

"Sooner than that, I'd wager." Gregor lowered his voice, "I cannot tell you here. Shall we find a more private place?"

She nodded. "The music room?"

"Very well. You go first," he instructed. Margarethe was curious about the wink Willem sent her way, but she preceded Gregor through the rowdy mob and toward the stairs.

Gregor followed, closing the door behind them and sinking wearily onto a stool at the table. "Ah, it is good to be home again."

For a moment she wondered if he would expect the kiss she had neglected to give him upon first greeting him. But he seemed content to sit and rest. And their kisses were unremarkable anyway, so she held her peace.

But what was this that could not be discussed in front of the others? She was curious.

"The war, Margarethe, my dear, may be over this coming week."

"But how? It would seem to be time for a siege now, and those are most tiresome and drawn out."

"True. But we will parley. Messengers have been sent to all

of our allies. If they all appear, it will be a most impressive sight, and Ewald will be hard put to resist. Your uncle arrives tomorrow, and my father will have him do the talking, as he is the best diplomat among us."

"You will go on this. . .excursion?"

"Yes. I am counted as one of the allies, as are my brothers."

"Oh, Gregor. I hope your plan is successful. I fear for you, for all of you. When you came close to taking that lance—" She shuddered, feeling the pain as if it were her own.

"It was not one of my best moments," he admitted, rubbing his side and wincing a little. "But I was spared—thanks largely to your prayers, my lady." He took her hand and smiled into her eyes. "You are the angel God has given to bring me safely through this war."

Margarethe forced a smile. How could that be—when her own heart did not bear witness to his?

He rose reluctantly. "We must get back to the hall. The men will be assembling shortly for further instructions about our venture later this week. But keep my secret, my lady. We need the element of surprise."

"Will you be armed?" she asked in a small voice.

"We will dress to make an impression, I can assure you. And we will take along a secret weapon." He grinned at her look of puzzlement.

"I will cover you with my prayers as always, but won't you please wear the mail hauberk underneath—just in case?"

At this, he tugged her into his arms and held her tightly. "For you, my lady, I would give my life."

Margarethe closed her eyes and yielded to his embrace. Perhaps—just perhaps—she could learn to love this man, after all.

⁂

At Mass on the Lord's Day, Margarethe was surprised to see Gregor, Willem, and Klaus dressed—not in mail—but in traveling clothes. She waited outside the chapel for them, hoping to find out what they were up to.

"An affair of state," was all Willem would confide when she asked. Klaus looked watchful and as stern as ever, but Gregor reserved his most tender smile for her. "Once more we'll need your prayers, my lady."

"And you shall have them." She eyed him suspiciously. "Are you wearing the mail under your tunic as you promised?"

At that moment, Gregor looked no older than little Friedrich now, and ducked his head in embarrassment. "I fear I forgot."

"The lady is wise," Willem put in. "We should pray as if everything depends upon God, and be as prudent as if everything depends upon ourselves."

"Hmmph!" Klaus snorted. "We're wasting time if we have to add the hauberk. But come, Willem. I have an extra that would fit you."

Seeing their haste to be off, Margarethe gave each of them a fond farewell. But Gregor held her a moment longer than the others, then gestured for her to follow him to his chamber.

She hesitated only a moment. After all, they were betrothed, and—if the mission failed—this might be the last time she would ever see him.

Inside, she could not resist a quick look around. The man surely needed a valet, even in these temporary quarters in his father's house. With no one to keep order here and lay out his garments, no wonder he had forgotten to put on all the necessary armor.

"Well, Greta, have you decided what we will be doing this day?" he asked, beginning to remove his outer clothing.

She averted her eyes, looking instead at the cluttered room and mentally rearranging the furnishings. "Since you chose not to arm yourself, I suspect you are not going into battle today but may be planning a rendezvous with some of your allies to persuade them to come parley with Ewald tomorrow. Am I right?"

He grinned. "Your reasoning is most admirable, my lady. Ewald will not be convinced to surrender if certain allies do not appear. Therefore, we need our very best diplomat."

"Well, then, that explains Klaus's part. Despite his morose attitude lately, he is known to be the best diplomat among you brothers. But what of Willem? He is not a soldier."

Gregor would not answer directly. "Trust me, my lady. He is needed. Now you must leave so I can prepare myself as you directed." He gave a little bow and pushed her toward the door. "But I have one last request. We will break our fast along the road. So don't come to see us off. We've said our farewells, and time is short."

She nodded, brushed her lips against his cheek and left the room. But when the three men mounted up to ride out of the courtyard, she was watching from her chamber window. Carefully strapped to the back of Willem's horse was a package the size of a lute.

She left her room to go to the chapel to pray, and did not emerge until dinnertime.

sixteen

When Margarethe went to the hall for dinner, she found that her aunt and uncle had arrived, along with young Friedrich. She laughed as she flew into her aunt's outstretched arms. "Oh, Aunt Mechthild, it feels like years since I've seen you! I've missed you so."

"Ah, Greta, you're looking well," said her uncle, giving her an assessing glance.

"Greta, when are you going to show me around this great big castle. It's the biggest castle I've ever seen!" Friedrich piped up. "I want to see everything! The secret hiding places and the dungeons and all the best ponds to catch frogs!"

There was a round of hearty laughter as they were escorted to the head table, where Jolan was already seated, waiting for them.

"From what Otto tells me, son," began Lord Einhard, sliding into the seat a page held for him, "Margarethe has been much too busy to explore her surroundings."

"True, Friedrich," she admitted. "When I first came here, I helped your sister Jolan care for a lady who had been sadly injured. And since Willem has been away with the troops, I've been helping with the music students."

"Did the sick lady get better?" The freckled face grew sober. "Or did she die?"

"She is quite well, I'm happy to report. Oh, and I took care of a wounded captain, who also recovered."

Friedrick was all ears. "What happened to him?"

"One of the enemy soldiers charged him with a lance. Unfortunately, our captain had neglected to wear his breastplate

154

that day."

"Then he should be dead," said Friedrich, philosophically.

Margarethe nodded. "And he likely would have been killed, too. But as it happened, the enemy soldier's horse slipped in the mud, and his lance only grazed the captain's side."

"Were you there?" Friedrich asked, obviously intent on learning every detail of the incident.

"Oh, no." Margarethe laughed at the earnest little face. "At least not in the flesh." She leaned closer to look him directly in the eye. "But your sister, the injured lady, and I were there in another way. We were praying at that very moment."

"And which of your fighting men was so lucky as to have your prayers?" asked Lady Mechthild.

"Gregor," Margarethe replied, lifting a mug of warmed cider to her lips..

"Oh, so it was your betrothed. How interesting. You must love him very much if you are so faithful to pray for him."

"Oh, Mutti," Jolan said, "they're always together. Gregor is in our Lord's Day musical group as well, along with Hilda and Albert and Willem."

"Fine musicians all," Lady Mechthild commented. "Do you play here in the hall as you did at Adlerschloss?"

"Of course," Jolan spoke up. "In fact, Margarethe and I will sing for you this very evening, if you like—though we've had no time to prepare for your coming," she said with a trace of reprimand in her voice.

Mechthild nodded, pleased. "So we surprised you, then, my dears?"

"Yes, and what a nice surprise," Margarethe said. "My own parents will be here soon for the betrothal feast, though they will leave my younger sister at home this trip. She prefers to wait for the wedding."

Friedrich made his voice heard from the other side of the

table. "When will I meet your father—the great man I am named after?"

"Very soon, child," Mechthild answered for Margarethe. "But you must keep quiet now. We have important matters to discuss."

Lord Einhard leaned over the table. "And where is Lord Gregor today, Margarethe? I was looking forward to seeing him."

"He is on some mission with Klaus. They will return very late tonight, he said."

"And I do not see Willem about, either," he remarked.

"They are together—on the same mission."

Lady Mechthild's eyebrows rose. "Gregor. . .and Willem? They get along well?"

"Oh, yes," Margarethe said, wickedly enjoying the growing alarm on her aunt's face. "They are probably best friends. Would you not agree, Jolan?"

"I would say so. They even bathe together," she said, bursting into laughter.

"Hmm. . .It must be some very important mission indeed," Einhard observed, "to send them out on the Lord's Day."

❧

Margarethe waited for the men's return, praying that nothing had gone amiss. When she heard the sound of horses' hooves clattering through the gate, she dressed hurriedly, left her chamber, and met them in the hallway.

"You are up late, my lady," Gregor said softly with a warning look she could make out even by torchlight. Klaus seemed miffed; Willem, triumphant.

"I waited up to see how you fared on your mysterious mission," she replied. "Were you successful?"

"Completely," Gregor replied. "Perhaps we will be able to tell you about it soon—but not tonight."

She couldn't hide her disappointment. "Uncle Einhard has

been looking forward to seeing you and was disappointed when he found you gone," she said, hoping Gregor would relent and share the news now.

"He will not be disappointed when he learns the whole story. But, Margarethe, it is late and we are spent. Thank you for your prayers."

She nodded, still wishing someone would tell her more. Why must men keep secrets? "Good night then, Gregor. Good night, Klaus, Willem. God bless you all."

Gregor pressed her hand to his lips, then left for his quarters. Klaus, too, bowed and passed by. Only Willem was left. "Do not ever stop praying, my lady," he said, taking her hand. "God was with us tonight, and I know your prayers had something to do with it."

"Then I will never stop."

Willem smiled and lifted the hand he was holding to kiss her fingers. "Good night, *Liebchen*," he whispered, brushed her cheek with the back of his hand, and went on.

Feeling more and more confused, Margarethe returned to her chamber, undressed, and got into bed. Willem had seemed so confident for the past few days—almost as if he were in a world of his own. He had even told her some fanciful tale about a cloth merchant—something Hilda had taught him. Then he had proceeded to baffle her even more by telling her he was thanking God for answering his prayers—even though there was no visible sign of the answer. Perhaps, after she and Gregor were wed, Willem would become a priest like Father Bernard. It did seem his thoughts were loftier these days, more focused on heavenly things.

Sleepless, she lay awake, pondering. Willem was praising God for something He had not brought to pass as yet. Was that the secret of prayer?

Here on the eve of her betrothal to Gregor, Willem might well have come to terms with the truth and changed his prayer to one of acceptance. But if he had not—if he were still praying for some miracle for them—she prayed fervently the Good Lord would answer. For if He did not and she married Gregor, Willem's faith might be shattered.

In four days, the betrothal would be accomplished. Only four days. God could still work a miracle. But she, too, ought to pray like Willem. She would try. She recited her list of family and friends—concentrating on their needs instead of hers. She prayed for wisdom and discernment, for an end to all war. For peace in her own troubled heart.

As dawn streaked the sky, trailing fingers of pink and purple, Margarethe at last gave up and prayed Willem's prayer. "Father, you know the prayer I have been praying since I met this man as a little girl. I thank You for hearing me. I thank You for hearing Willem's prayers. You have been so faithful to answer other prayers, and I know You are answering this one as well. Perhaps not as we would hope—but Your ways are best and right. I praise You for being a good and loving God, One who knows what we need—even if we do not always get what we want."

She continued thanking and praising God until she fell asleep, completely content as she had not been in many months.

☙

On Tuesday morning, at the shout of the lookout in the turret, Margarethe ran to her window to find a large mounted party approaching from the west. Hurriedly tucking her errant hair under her cap, she ran down the stairs.

"Greta, you must let me dress your hair," Aunt Mechthild said, half scolding. "There is yet time before Friedrich and Ida are within the castle walls. Your mother must not see you in a little girl's cap."

Margarethe could not resist a teasing retort. "It keeps my head warm, Aunt."

"Back up the stairs with you now. I'm sure you brought something we can use."

Margarethe allowed her aunt to rebraid her long blond hair and select a becoming veil. Today she had chosen her second best gown—a dove gray tunic with a murrey surcoat. Margarethe liked murrey; it reminded her of berries.

Putting the finishing touches on the new hairstyle, her aunt anchored the veil with a gold circlet studded with garnets. "There now, you look more like a young lady who is soon to wed—and not a naughty child tormenting her poor old aunt." Lady Mechthild chuckled fondly.

Skimming the stairs to greet her parents in the hallway below, Margarethe embraced them, then stood back so that they could get a good look at her—and she at them. It had been so long. Her parents seemed somehow much smaller than she remembered them. Papa's hair was touched with silver at the temples, and Mutti—well, when she spoke, her voice held the same lovely rich timbre Margarethe recalled as a child when her mother had sung lullabies at bedtime.

"You are grown, my little Greta," she said, holding Margarethe at arm's length. "Taller than your Mutti. And to think, you are soon to be a bride."

The thought was less than reassuring.

❧

"Mutti, let us make music together as we used to do," Margarethe suggested just before supper. "Aunt Mechthild is anxious for us to entertain, and we might provide a diversion from thoughts of this never-ending war."

"Ever thoughtful," Lady Ida said, patting her daughter's hand.

"Hmm. Yes," her father muttered fondly. "Ever thoughtful—unless she's playing a joke on someone." His smile removed any sting his words might have caused. "Am I invited to make music with you ladies?"

"Of course you are, Papa. Come and help me carry some things." He accompanied her up the stairs and to the music room, where Margarethe chose an assortment of wind instruments and put them in a bag, then took up her lute and a viel and bow.

He frowned. "Will you promise me not to let Mechthild play that thing?" he asked as he eyed the viel with misgiving.

Margarethe laughed. "So her fame on the viel reaches even to the Schwarzwald."

"Her infamy, more like," he said as he took up the bag and the lute. "Has anyone heard from Otto?"

"I have heard nothing yet. The parley was to last only one day, though." Despite her prayers, this comment triggered a spark of terror. What if negotiations failed? And now she had not one man to worry about—but two.

They descended the stairs together in silence.

"This delay is unnerving," her father continued. "We should be hearing something. Still, I cannot picture Otto in peacetime. It seems unnatural somehow. After all, this conflict has gone on for the past twenty years. I suppose war is a way of life for him."

Margarethe couldn't help thinking that perhaps Lord Otto had changed his mind and decided there should be no truce at all. Or maybe they were all being held hostage. . . For a dreadful moment, her faith faltered, and a thousand horrors came to mind.

ঌ

On Wednesday Margarethe rose early for Mass. There were more people than usual on their knees this morning, likely praying for peace, as she was, and for the men who had gone to make the peace. She tried to pray without fretting, but there had been no word at all, and her natural instincts rose up to crowd her mind.

Lady Edeltraud had considered sending a messenger to find

out what was happening, but she dared not do anything that
Ewald might construe as a hostile act. And so they had
waited.

During the mass Margarethe decided to use her new
method of prayer—the one Willem had taught her. Doing her
best to put her fears aside, she praised God, thanking Him for
all that He had already done for them—Gregor's escape from
certain death; Hilda's healing, both physical and mental; her
growing friendship with Gregor, her love for Willem and the
miracle they desired—if, in truth, such a miracle was best for
all concerned.

As she prayed, a small kernel of joy began deep within and
bubbled to the surface until she felt that she would burst.
"Bless Willem, Father. And Gregor and Klaus and Uncle
Einhard—especially Uncle, for he is to be doing the talking
today. Bring them home safely. . .and bring peace."

₰

With the preparations for the betrothal feast and the antici-
pated homecoming of the fighting men in full swing, the castle was abuzz with activity. Once again, Hilda must be moved
to accommodate the many guests who would be arriving
soon, it was hoped.

"We keep moving you about, Hilda," Jolan said while helping her relocate from the private chamber she had occupied
for only a short time back into Jolan's chamber. "I do hope
you don't feel neglected or unwanted."

Hilda laughed her gentle laugh. "Not at all. I know you
care for me. You've proven it in a thousand ways."

Margarethe winced. "I feel guilty, for I have had my own
chamber all along."

Jolan gave an exaggerated sigh. "Don't remind me.
However, since you are the guest of honor here, I suppose we
must concede. Even the lords are doubling up to make room."

"I wonder what poor soul will have to share Gregor's

chamber," Margarethe mused.

Hilda covered her mouth with her hand, her eyes wide and Margarethe realized too late how her remark must have sounded.

Jolan straightened and gave her a searching look. "In just a few months *you* will be that poor soul. And what would be so bad about sharing with Gregor anyway?"

"Nothing, if he had his valet with him here. He sorely needs one. He leaves his clothes strewn about everywhere," Margarethe explained.

"Oh," Jolan said slyly. "I thought perhaps he snored."

"Now what," Margarethe demanded, "would I know about that?"

"Then how do you know how he keeps his chamber?"

"Please don't quarrel," Hilda begged, with a look of alarm on her face. "It serves no purpose."

"Ha! If you think we are quarreling now, you should have seen us when we were younger."

"I remember wishing I had a sister—or a very close cousin," Hilda said thoughtfully. "Perhaps it would not have been so wonderful, after all."

That brought an end to the chiding as Margarethe and Jolan erupted in gales of laughter.

"I have a younger sister that I barely know," Margarethe said, suddenly serious. "I am looking forward to seeing her. . .at the wedding." But she was not looking forward to the wedding.

❧

In the afternoon, Margarethe and her aunt and mother had called their own truce over the garments she would wear for the betrothal feast—a purple tunic with bands on the sleeves, embroidered by her mother, and a light blue diapered cloth surcoat her aunt had had made. Since she herself favored the colors, everyone would be satisfied.

With that decision behind, Margarethe was eager to get on

with a more pleasant activity—a family musical concert. They were playing their second number—a driving dance tune called an estampie—when a general stirring in the hall outside reached her ears, and she laid aside her viel and bow.

Gregor was the first man through the door. He strode over, lifted her off her feet, and swung her in a circle. "Ewald has surrendered, my lady! Unconditionally!"

"Oh, Gregor, my heart is so full," she cried, "of gratitude for God's goodness in sparing you and the others."

"It might have gone either way, had it not been for your prayers." Noticing the little group gathered around, he turned to greet them. "Forgive me. These must be your parents, Margarethe. You resemble your mother—a legendary beauty indeed. Lady Ida." He bowed over her hand.

Her mother dimpled, her eyes twinkling. "And you're much more dashing and distinguished than when you were a boy."

Margarethe could not help thinking that perhaps Gregor should be the family diplomat—not Klaus, who was always so dour

At that moment Lord Friedrich stepped up to extend his hand, sizing Gregor up in a single look, she observed. Her father would not be able to find anything to fault in Gregor, she thought. Nothing except his housekeeping, at least.

"So this is the young lord who will marry my daughter," her father said, still skeptical, or so it appeared.

Gregor smiled and would have replied except Lady Mechthild spoke up just then. "I must find Einhard," she said, rising from her chair. "Oh, there he is now."

When Lord Einhard strode over to greet them, it was Gregor who spoke first. "Here is the hero of the parley. Never have I seen such courage and persistence."

Lord Einhard clapped Gregor on the shoulder as he passed him to embrace his wife, and then his sister, Lady Ida and

Lord Friedrich. "I must confess I never worked any harder on the battlefield. But—"

Glancing toward the door, Margarethe saw Willem enter just as her uncle finished his statement, "There is the real hero."

※

All of the lords attending the parley and their allies sent messengers to their homes with the good news, called for their families to join them at the castle, then stayed for supper, with music and dancing far into the night. Margarethe had never before observed such a sight. She herself, caught up in the excitement, was a part of many of the musical presentations. And she noticed that her cousin Jolan—when she was not playing an instrument—danced every dance, most notably with two of their young allies, Lord Selig and Lord Helmhold.

Throughout the evening, Margarethe sang often, blending her voice with others in a variety of performances. Once she sang a solo. And when someone called for the love song she had written, she felt a bittersweet pang as she sang in harmony with Willem, feeling his gaze resting on her tenderly. There was a request for the war song, but Willem refused, and Margarethe wondered why.

He shrugged. "It is Lord Otto's idea. I am to play it tomorrow."

She smiled weakly at him. "Instead of the betrothal music you were to write?"

"In addition to that," he said, smiling broadly.

Before she could press him further, Gregor claimed her for a dance, and she whirled away, looking back over her shoulder at Willem. He was a puzzlement to her. How could he appear so cheerful on the very eve of her betrothal to another?

It was quite late when she finally retired, but she could not fall asleep right away. Strangely though, in thinking of the morrow, she felt neither fearful nor sad. Instead, she spent some time in prayer, thanking and praising God before a gentle blanket of peace descended over her, and she slept.

❧

After Mass, Margarethe could not find Jolan anywhere. She looked all over the castle, then returned to Jolan's chamber. "Hilda, have you seen my cousin?"

"I think she went somewhere with Willem. Do you need her?"

"Well, I need someone. This hair is too much for me alone. I am to wear it loose for the feast, so I need to wash it right away, else it will not dry. Aunt Mechthild is nowhere to be seen." She waggled her fingers in the air. "Besides that, my father is in some meeting with Uncle Einhard and Lord Otto and Gregor. I don't know what is going on. I would have thought they'd have had everything settled by now."

Hilda seemed to be ignoring her perplexity. "Is the water ready?" she asked in her calm way.

At her words Margarethe was brought back to her current quandary. "Oh, I asked for it last night to be sure they would bring it this morning."

"Then let me help," Hilda offered. "You have such lovely hair that it would be a pleasure."

When her hair was thoroughly clean, Margarethe sat with her back to the window, her head in the direct sunlight. "Perhaps we should take the longest part of your hair and toss it out the window to dry the quicker," Hilda suggested with a smile.

"And if a bird chances upon it, we will have to start over. No. I think not, Hilda."

"You seem quite happy, Margarethe. You must have grown to love Lord Gregor very much."

A long look passed between them. "Let's just say I am at peace. God's in His heaven, and all is well." How she *knew* such a thing mystified her, but she was confident that it was true.

"I will be praying for you today. It is too bad that the peace treaty had to come at the same time as your betrothal announcement. It will not get as much attention as it deserves—as *you* deserve."

"I don't mind." Margarethe had never felt so certain of anything in her life. "It is peace that is the most important thing."

ॐ

Gregor was Margarethe's dinner partner, a novelty only in that she had not seen him all morning. During the last course, he took her hand. "I want you to know that I truly admire you, my lady."

She narrowed her gaze in speculation. "Well, thank you, my lord. But I would find it rather odd if you found your future wife *objectionable*."

As soon as the tables were cleared, the herald quieted the hall for Lord Otto. Margarethe had never seen the man looking so jovial. Gone was the fierce, almost menacing countenance. He was actually smiling, which gave him a different appearance altogether.

"As you know, after a long and valiant struggle, we are at peace." He waited for the cheers to subside before outlining the terms of the peace agreement. "If all abide by these terms, we should enjoy many years of tranquility and prosperity within our borders."

Margarethe drummed her fingers on the table until Gregor covered her hand with his own. After-dinner speeches were so boring. Would her future father-in-law just conclude the business so they could get back to their musicmaking?

"Now for the business at hand. There is one man in particular I wish to honor here this day. A man who never took up arms, but one whose skills and encouragement have led us to this moment."

To Margarethe's surprise, Lord Otto turned to look at

Willem, sitting at the end of the table. "Willem, will you honor this hall with the battle song that brought us victory?"

Willem nodded, made his way to the front, and sang the stirring words that told of courageous deeds done in the name of love and loyalty, with the help of Almighty God.

At the conclusion of the verses, the men joined in the chorus, their strong masculine voices filling the place with rich sound. Once more the herald was called to quiet the hall before Lord Otto could speak. "After due deliberation," he began, "my sons and I have decided to reward this hero."

A great shout went up as the fighting men confirmed the decision with their cheers, and Margarethe glanced at Gregor, whose eyes were moist.

"The only reward our chief musician would accept was a small plot of land," Lord Otto went on. "But in view of his unique contribution to our cause, we have decided that in addition to the land, he should be given a fitting dwelling as well." Once again the hall erupted in shouts and cheers. When the applause had died down, he finished, "And so I give you Lord Willem of Waldbergen Castle!"

Margarethe sat, stunned, as the fighting men of Lord Otto's household stood to their feet and launched into another chorus of the battle song. Gregor, she observed, remained seated, too, leaning forward to make a comment. "He is a true nobleman—as gallant and brave as any knight."

Tears filled her eyes. She was happy for Willem, but his land had come too late. Her betrothal to Gregor was to be announced this very day. She could not dishonor Gregor when he had been nothing but kind to her.

"Our announcement pales by comparison," she said, bravely trying to meet his eye.

He shook his head. "We need make no announcement, dear Greta."

She frowned, trying to understand. "But my parents have

come all the way from the Schwarzwald for the occasion."

"They came for the announcement of your betrothal, my lady."

Was he mad? "That is what I just said, Gregor."

"No, you said something about *our* announcement." When she continued to stare, uncomprehendingly, he said, "I care for you deeply, but are we not more like brother and sister? You deserve a man who truly loves you—and here he comes now." He nodded toward Willem, who was walking toward them with that endearing bouncing gait. "And so I release you from our betrothal."

She turned to Willem as he bent to speak with her. "Your uncle and Gregor did battle for me, and your father and Lord Otto are agreed. All I need now is your consent, my lady. Do I have it? Will you marry me?"

Through a veil of tears, she saw the dear face she had adored since she was but a girl of eleven. "I will, my lord." She stepped into his arms, and he kissed her tenderly, to the great delight of the hall.

Gregor, standing to the side, beamed his approval. "You both have my blessings," he said. Then stepping back, he announced, "Now I have work to do, if you will excuse me."

Margarethe sat down again, with Willem at her side clasping her hand tightly. He sang softly in her ear:

> 'Til all our days shall pass,
>   We'll be together, you and me,
> As ever on the brook flows down
>   Constant to the sea.
> As it's renewed by snow and rain
>   Our love's fed from above.
> I always will be true to you—

"Oh, Willem," she cried, "and you'll always be my love!

Our prayer and our song have both come true, haven't they?

She turned to see Gregor, Albert, Jolan, and Aunt Mechthild taking their places at the front of the dais, where they performed a merry piece Margarethe had never heard.

"Our betrothal music," Willem explained. "The inspiration came soon enough when I knew that *I* would be your betrothed."

"So that is why you've been so happy of late." She gazed at him with wonder and admiration. "When did you write this music?"

"A fortnight ago."

"So you have known all this time about your land?" she asked.

"Oh, no. I learned about that only this morning."

"I still don't understand. How did you know a fortnight ago that you would be my betrothed?"

"That is when I began to thank God for what He was doing for us. He gave me such joy. Then these past few days I have seen the same joy shining in your eyes, and it gave me even more hope."

They sat smiling at each other as the song ended and the hall erupted in loud applause. "I will have to listen to that song sometime—when I can truly hear every word," Margarethe murmured.

Lord Otto stood to his feet to make the betrothal announcement—quite different from the original one planned. Margarethe's heart was full as she and Willem rose to acknowledge the good wishes of the audience—dear family and friends all.

"So this was your prayer," Hilda said when at last she could make her way to the happy couple.

"Yes," they said in unison. "And God bless you for praying, Hilda."

"I thank you, too, for the story about the merchant," Willem said, nestling Margarethe closer to his side.

And then Gregor was back to hug each of them in turn. "I know of no two people who deserve greater happiness," he said graciously. "You're a fortunate man, my friend."

Safe in Willem's embrace, Margarethe put her hand on Gregor's arm and, cocking her head, said in a mischievous tone, "I have a little sister at home, my lord. And she's nothing at all like me!"

Gregor's grin lit up the vast hall. "So your father tells me," he said. "So your father tells me."

A Letter To Our Readers

Dear Reader:

In order that we might better contribute to your reading enjoyment, we would appreciate your taking a few minutes to respond to the following questions. When completed, please return to the following:

Rebecca Germany, Managing Editor
Heartsong Presents
PO Box 719
Uhrichsville, Ohio 44683

1. Did you enjoy reading *For a Song?*
   ❑ Very much. I would like to see more books
      by this author!
   ❑ Moderately
      I would have enjoyed it more if _____

   _____

2. Are you a member of **Heartsong Presents**? ❑Yes ❑No
   If no, where did you purchase this book?_____

   _____

3. What influenced your decision to purchase this
   book? (Check those that apply.)

   ❑ Cover   ❑ Back cover copy

   ❑ Title   ❑ Friends

   ❑ Publicity   ❑ Other_____

4. How would you rate, on a scale from 1 (poor) to 5
   (superior), the cover design?_____

5. On a scale from 1 (poor) to 10 (superior), please rate the following elements.

    ___Heroine   ___Plot

    ___Hero   ___Inspirational theme

    ___Setting   ___Secondary characters

6. What settings would you like to see covered in **Heartsong Presents** books?_____

    _____

    _____

7. What are some inspirational themes you would like to see treated in future books?_____

    _____

    _____

8. Would you be interested in reading other **Heartsong Presents** titles?   ❑ Yes   ❑ No

9. Please check your age range:
    ❑ Under 18   ❑ 18-24   ❑ 25-34
    ❑ 35-45   ❑ 46-55   ❑ Over 55

10. How many hours per week do you read? _____

Name _____

Occupation_____

Address_____

City_____ State_____ Zip_____

········ Presents ········

Great Inspirational Romance at a Great Price!

Heartsong Presents books are inspirational romances in contemporary and historical settings, designed to give you an enjoyable, spirit-lifting reading experience. You can choose wonderfully written titles from some of today's best authors like Peggy Darty, Sally Laity, Tracie Peterson, Colleen L. Reece, Lauraine Snelling, and many others.

When ordering quantities less than twelve, above titles are $2.95 each.
Not all titles may be available at time of order.

SEND TO: Heartsong Presents Reader's Service
P.O. Box 719, Uhrichsville, Ohio 44683

Please send me the items checked above. I am enclosing $_____.
(please add $1.00 to cover postage per order. OH add 6.25% tax. NJ add 6%). Send check or money order, no cash or C.O.D.s, please.
To place a credit card order, call 1-800-847-8270.

NAME _____

ADDRESS _____

CITY/STATE_____ ZIP _____

Heartsong Presents
Love Stories Are Rated G!

That's for godly, gratifying, and of course, great! If you love a thrilling love story, but don't appreciate the sordidness of some popular paperback romances, **Heartsong Presents** is for you. In fact, **Heartsong Presents** is the *only inspirational romance book club*, the only one featuring love stories where Christian faith is the primary ingredient in a marriage relationship.

Sign up today to receive your first set of four, never before published Christian romances. Send no money now; you will receive a bill with the first shipment. You may cancel at any time without obligation, and if you aren't completely satisfied with any selection, you may return the books for an immediate refund!

Imagine. . .four new romances every four weeks—two historical, two contemporary—with men and women like you who long to meet the one God has chosen as the love of their lives. . .all for the low price of $9.97 postpaid.

To join, simply complete the coupon below and mail to the address provided. **Heartsong Presents** romances are rated G for another reason: They'll arrive *Godspeed!*